HOPE SPRINGS A LEAK

Ted Staunton

Red Deer College Press

Northern Lights Young Novels are published by
Red Deer College Press
56 Avenue & 32 Street Box 5005
Red Deer Alberta Canada T4N 5H5

Acknowledgments
Edited for the Press by Peter Carver
Cover illustration by Kasia Charko
Cover design by Boldface Technologies Inc.
Printed and bound in Canada by WebCom for Red Deer College Press

Financial support provided by the Alberta Foundation for the Arts, a beneficiary of the Lottery Fund of the Government of Alberta, and by the Canada Council, the Department of Canadian Heritage and Red Deer College.

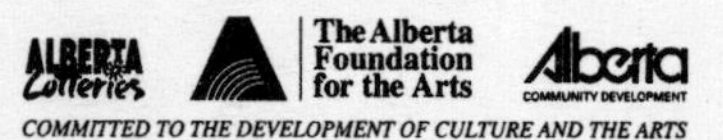

The Canada Council for the Arts since 1957
Le Conseil des Arts du Canada depuis 1957

Canadian Cataloguing in Publication
Staunton, Ted, 1956–
Hope springs a leak
(Northern lights young novels)
ISBN 0-88995-174-8
I. Title. II. Series.
PS8587.T334H66 1998 jC813'.54 C98-910250-5
PZ7.S8076Ho 1998

5 4 3 2 1

*To my family and all our
friends in Hope Springs*

The author gratefully acknowledges the editorial assistance of Peter Carver.

Contents

1
The Bulging Bin

Something was wrong with Sam Foster's pants. Sam hadn't really noticed when he'd first pulled on his favorite jeans after school. They'd been a little tight maybe, but he expected that with jeans fresh from the wash. Besides, he'd been in a hurry to get to the Bulging Bin bulk food store and start his chores. It was the second day of grade six, and Sam's new teacher had said she'd be dropping by on her way home. Sam wanted to be there, looking sharp. Ms. Broom had made a big impression.

Sam's teacher was brand new at O.P. Doberman School. She seemed quite young for a grownup—and friendly. Ms. Broom had short, dark hair, attractive wire-rimmed glasses, and a fetching smile with an astonishing number of very white teeth. In a word, she was—well, Sam didn't actually have a word for what she was. Even if he had, he was pretty sure it would have been an embarrassing one. So, instead, Sam thought more about how Ms. Broom had Maple Leafs and Blue Jays posters up in her classroom and let you read the newspaper—including the comics—if your work was done. It seemed safer, somehow.

All the way to the store, Sam had thought about what he'd be doing and what he'd say when Ms. Broom arrived. Now though, doing his chores, his pants were driving him crazy. There was a lump beneath his bottom and part way down one leg. Whatever it was (Sam didn't want to think too much about that part), it was making the jeans so tight he could hardly walk. This hadn't been in his plans for looking cool.

Sam wiggled as he swept the floor, trying to shift the mystery lump. His broom veered wildly; but the lump didn't budge.

"Whatta ya doin'?" Sam's best friend Darryl Sweeney was idling by the candy bins, holding his newspaper carrier bag, and waiting for Sam to finish.

Sam discreetly probed his rear. The lump was large and definitely squishy. Several alarming possibilities flashed through his brain. "Something's in there," he confessed.

A lady at the spices glanced at him sharply and moved away.

"Gross," Darryl said. "What is it?"

"I dunno." Sam gingerly slipped a hand down the back of his jeans until it bumped into what felt like a bundle of cloth. He scissored his fingers, trying to snag it.

Suddenly a voice boomed behind him. "You lose something in there or just keeping warm?" Sam jumped and dropped his broom. A short, bald-headed man with bristling eyebrows stood watching him with interest.

"Yessir," Sam fumbled, pulling out his hand. "I mean, no. I mean, I dunno . . ." He had recognized his questioner right away. It was J. Earl Goodenough, Hope Springs' most famous citizen.

"Smart idea, keeping warm," J. Earl said, nodding authoritatively. J. Earl always said what he thought. He had written all kinds of books, and he was on TV a lot, too, telling what he thought. What he thought, mainly, was that things were dumb. "Darned air conditioning. I hate air conditioning. Makes me too cold—then I get overheated thinking about it."

Sam was puzzling this out when J. Earl said, "Work here, do ya? What's your name?"

"Yes," Sam said, "I mean, I'm Sam Foster. This is my mom's store."

"I'll remember that," said J. Earl. "Never forget a name.

What I do forget is my glasses. What does that say? My wife writes too small."

He handed a paper to Sam, who read out, "Baking soda." Sam pointed. "It's over there."

"Good man, Foster," J. Earl said, and stalked away. Darryl popped a sympathetic gum bubble. "Looks better on TV."

Sam nodded, still a little shaken by his brush with greatness. He bent to pick up his broom and was reminded again of the mystery lump. He looked around. "Hey, stand in front of me."

Darryl obligingly blocked the aisle while Sam thrust his hand back down his jeans. This time he latched onto the cloth and tugged. His pants were too snug to budge it. "Ah, geez!"

With his free hand, Sam reached hastily under the long, white apron he always wore in the store and unbuttoned the top of his jeans. He hoped his mother wasn't watching this up at the cash. The loosened waist wasn't enough. He undid his fly as well, and the seat of his pants went slack. Clutching his waistband, Sam pushed deeper, grabbed the lump of cloth, and pulled out—

"Hey, look!" Darryl cried. "Here comes Ms. Broom!"

"What?" Sam looked up wildly. Their lovely new teacher was coming through the door. She saw the boys and waved. Automatically, Sam raised a hand to wave back. His jeans slid to his ankles. At the same moment he saw that he was also clutching a knot of white cloth. It was three pairs of freshly laundered underpants.

"Omigawd." He shoved the underpants at the startled Darryl.

"Eeww," Darryl said, and shoved them right back. Sam flailed frantically to pull up his jeans. As Ms. Broom approached, Sam did the only thing he could think of: he tossed the underwear over his shoulder as far as he could.

"Hey!" An angry shout erupted from the opposite aisle. It was followed by a hissing sound, like sand running through fingers. Yanking his pants up, Sam peered over the bulk

almonds. J. Earl Goodenough had two pairs of underpants on his shiny head and a bagful of baking soda all over the rest of him.

"Holy mackerel," Darryl said helpfully.

J. Earl's head flushed a deep red. His massive eyebrows flapped and his nostrils flared, the way they did when he got worked up on TV. "I'll remember this," he said, as Sam's mom came bustling up to see what was the matter.

"Sorry," Sam said weakly. His white apron was billowing like a waterfall out of the unfastened front of his jeans. Above him, he saw the third pair of underpants dangling from the light fixture. Behind him, he heard a noise that could only be described as a snort. He turned. Ms. Broom was struggling valiantly not to laugh. Sam looked from his glaring mom to his amused teacher to the sulfurous J. Earl. Then and there he decided it was time for a new Sam Foster.

2

Unfriendly Neighbors

"He didn't have to be *that* mad," Sam complained at dinner that night. Really he was more upset about looking foolish in front of Ms. Broom, but he didn't want to say that. It was easier to gripe about J. Earl Goodenough.

"That's his job, Sammy," his dad said. "People like it when J. Earl sounds off because it's what they'd like to do themselves."

"Yeah, but what if he tells about me on TV? The whole world will think I'm stupid!"

"It already does," muttered Sam's sister, Robin.

"Not the *whole* world," Sam said. It wasn't quite what he meant.

"Well, Sam, I just want you to know that you've wrecked it for me," Robin said. Robin was in grade eleven and often grumpy, especially when Mr. Foster made Lentils Supreme for dinner.

"How?" Sam was affronted. "It wasn't your underwear."

Robin glared. "Ha, ha, ha. Mrs. Goldenrod says *I* have to go to J. Earl Goodenough's *house* and interview him for media class. If he knows you're my brother he won't let us in the door."

"He won't anyway," said Sam. "I bet he hates orange hair." Robin's hair had recently become orange, except where she'd shaved it off.

"Enough," said Mrs. Foster. "When's the interview and who is 'us'?"

"Me and Marlon." Marlon was Robin's boyfriend. He had orange hair, too, and a nostril ring. "It's in three weeks. He picks the day."

"Maybe he'll have forgotten by then."

"Nope," Sam said. "He said he'd remember." He had a feeling Ms. Broom would, too.

"Oh great!" sighed Robin and Mrs. Foster, but then Mrs. Foster didn't care for Lentils Supreme, either.

Sam decided to try to forget the whole thing. It was hard enough just trying to become a new person. In a little town like Hope Springs, everyone pretty much knew you already. People were skeptical of sudden changes. Also, it was hard to be cool when your best friend was telling everyone how you'd thrown your underwear onto a famous man's head.

On the other hand, as Sam soon realized, this act had made him famous, too, in a small way. To his relief, Ms. Broom never mentioned it, but a lot of kids at school did. They seemed to think he'd done it on purpose. Several grade fours even wanted Sam to throw some more underwear at the principal. Obviously, tossing your underpants around could seem daring as well as dumb. Sam wondered briefly if he had the makings of a class clown. Maybe he would start a trend. For several days he watched the evening news, hoping that J. Earl would appear, sounding off about punk kids chucking their jockey shorts around. The great man never did, however, and when Sam couldn't think of any other riotous things to do, he gave up the idea of becoming funny.

He was at a loss until he happened to glance in the window of Grandstand Sports and Collectibles. The Grandstand sat just down the street from the Bulging Bin. There, on a hanger, hung a genuine Toronto Maple Leafs sweater, complete with the number of Sam's favorite player, Calvin "Truck" Mahoney.

It followed that anyone wearing the sweater would automatically acquire the nickname, too. Truck Foster. What could be cooler, thought Sam. He could almost hear the admirers already: "Here comes the Truck!" and "Keep on Truckin'!"

Best of all, it was clear Ms. Broom loved sports. Not only did she have team posters up in class, she had a sports watch, too. Lately, she had even been wearing a warm-up suit and had gone jogging at lunchtime. Sam saw instantly that someone wearing a genuine Leafs sweater would not only be cool in general, they'd be someone special to Ms. Broom. He hurried into the store.

Amanda Torrance was behind the counter, listening to the ball game on the radio. It was fitting that her family owned a sports store: Amanda was the best athlete in grade six.

"Hi, Sam," she said. "Wanta go play some catch?"

"I can't right now," Sam said. "How much is the Leafs sweater?"

"Just a sec," said Amanda. *"Da–ad!* How much is the Truck sweater?"

Sam glowed.

Mr. Torrance came out of the stock room, peering over his bifocals. He said hello to Sam and checked the price. It was expensive, too expensive for Sam to buy with just his allowance and his small wages from the Bin. Still, Mr. Torrance agreed to set it aside for a small down payment and the right to keep it in the store window.

Sam beetled off, first to the bank for the down payment, and then to the office of *The Hope Springs Eternal,* the town newspaper. It had been advertising for a paper boy just the day before. He was in luck. Even with the paper route job, it would take a while to buy the sweater, but it was a start. In the meantime, Sam decided, he'd have to do his best to impress the world any way he could.

The paper route started on Monday, so on the weekend, Darryl, who already delivered the *Eternal,* came over to share some of the finer points of the trade.

"First thing ya gotta know is how to fold them, Sam." Darryl demonstrated. "The way I do it is I hold it with my left hand, and then I use the first two fingers on my right hand to grab it, but only the edge, see, and then . . ." Darryl talked for several more minutes. All he really did was tuck one corner of the paper under the middle fold at the other side and press the whole thing flat. "See? It's tricky." Darryl always made things he knew about seem like rocket science. On the other hand, he always shared chocolate bars.

On Monday after school, a bundle of newspapers was waiting for Sam on the front porch, along with a dirty canvas carrier bag. He had a glass of milk, then set off with his route list.

The red *Eternal* carrier bag had a broad shoulder strap that made the weight of twenty-three papers just comfortable. Putting it on made Sam feel very professional. He slung the bag over to one side, so the white lettering showed, and slouched off down the street as if he'd been delivering papers all his life. Truck Foster, News Guy, he thought to himself. He was so busy thinking it, he almost missed the first address on his list.

Sam stopped and folded the paper the way Darryl had shown him. The *Eternal* was only a few pages long, and as Sam suspected, it was easy to do. Still, he did it carefully. It had occurred to him that a certain teacher might be among his customers.

A short way along his route he turned onto Albert Street. Hope Springs was a town of hills and old trees, and Albert Street was no exception. At the top of the hill, Sam left a paper at the Doberman mansion, home of the town's richest family, then moved down to Number 18, a small, neatly kept house with green trim. On the lawn just past it, a survey crew was pounding stakes into the ground under a big red maple. A familiar looking figure stood on Number 18's front step, watching them. Sam groaned. The figure jerked in recognition.

"You!" said J. Earl Goodenough as Sam approached. "Since when are you the paper boy?"

"Since today," Sam said.

"What happened to the other kid?" J. Earl didn't wait for an answer. "That's the trouble with alla you these days, you don't stick with anything. I used to have to yell at that kid nearly every day, always puttin' the paper in the wrong place, then she ups and quits for no reason. And she's not the only one. I'll bet she was the fifth this year. What's wrong with ya?"

Sam said, "Maybe she had too much homework." It wasn't the reason he had in mind.

"Hah!" J. Earl snorted. "In *my* day they gave homework. I never did it, but it was good for ya. Kids today have it soft. I'll bet you don't even have homework!"

"I do too," Sam said.

"Then why aren't you home doing it?" J. Earl absently dropped the unopened paper into a blue recycling box by the door and strode off toward the surveyors, barking, "So is it my tree? It better be!"

Sam sighed and moved on. Past the maple tree was a much larger house with an in-ground swimming pool nestled beside it. A silver-haired man in colorful golfing clothes was sitting on the broad front porch. The combination of house and hair and clothes was not uncommon. Hope Springs was a place a lot of city folk retired to.

The man rose politely and introduced himself as Mr. Cornell Leamish. "Don't let J. Earl Goodenough bother you," he said. "The other carriers quit because of him. We won't want to lose you. I can tell you're going to be good."

Sam wasn't sure how Cornell Leamish could tell that on his very first day. Maybe he *did* seem new and improved. Anyway, it was nicer than getting yelled at.

"Oh, I won't quit," Sam said, thinking about his Leafs sweater.

"Good," Cornell Leamish smiled. "I'm not a quitter, either. Maybe between the two of us we'll lick him." He glanced over at the men under the tree and his face darkened. Sam knew just how he felt; he'd had enough of J. Earl for one day.

As he got back to the street, though, there came a voice.

"Say, Foster!" J. Earl called, "You don't have a sister do you?" Sam nodded and something very heavy landed in his stomach. "Is she anything like you?"

Sam said, "No, she has orange hair," and headed downhill fast.

3
In the Deep End

It seemed better not to mention J. Earl at home just yet; having your older sister mad at you could be dangerous. Sam knew this from a trick he'd done once with toads and Robin's underwear drawer. Instead, he checked with Darryl.

"Hey, what do you do about crabby customers?"

"Keep away from 'em. Ya gotta be either really fast or really quiet," Darryl advised, sharing out some chocolate bar. "Watch out for dogs, too. The little yappy ones are the worst."

Sam couldn't imagine Darryl being fast *or* quiet in his clunky basketball shoes, but the next day, Sam practically tiptoed up to Goodenough's. Unfortunately, while J. Earl had complained about leaving the paper in the wrong place, he never had said where the right place was. Sam tucked it under the door mat, not noticing the puddle there until it was too late.

J. Earl caught him the next afternoon quietly struggling to fit the paper into the letter box. "Yesterday's paper looked like a dishrag, Foster. And this one's ripped. From now on put it in the right place!"

He pitched the torn paper disgustedly into the recycling again and slammed the door as Sam cried, "But where—"

Red-faced, Sam stalked back to the street. Cornell Leamish was under the maple tree, looking grimly at the survey stakes. They put the tree on J. Earl's property. Sam handed him his *Eternal*.

"Thank you," said Cornell Leamish. He started back to his

house, slapping his paper against his yellow golf slacks. Then he turned.

"Say," he said, "if you and your friends ever want to use the pool, you're welcome to—as long as I'm home, of course."

"Gee," Sam said.

"I had it built for my grandchildren," Cornell Leamish said. "But they've moved to Vancouver. It seems a shame not use it more."

"Thanks," said Sam, still a little stunned by this sudden good fortune. "We'll probably be over for sure."

With the warm summer weather hanging on, all Sam had to do was mention the word *pool* at school the next day. He made sure to do it in front of Ms. Broom. Sam half-hoped she might want to come swimming, too. She didn't, or didn't say so anyway. Lots of kids were definitely impressed, though. Truck Foster was rolling.

A good number of Sam's friends came along, including Darryl and Amanda. Sam hurried his paper route so he wouldn't be late. Nonetheless, he was overtaken on Albert Street by an impressively tall lady in khaki shorts who was striding briskly along the road. Sam had seen her walking in many places around town.

"Got a paper there for the Goodenoughs? I'll take it. I'm Mrs." Her tone was brisk, too. Mrs. Goodenough's was a voice used to giving orders. Still, it was friendly, with a pleasant growl to it that must have come from years of smoking.

Sam nodded and fumbled out an *Eternal.*

"It'll save you looking for the right place to put it. Or have you found it?"

Sam shook his head. Mrs. Goodenough looked amused.

"Well, keep looking. And don't worry, his bark is worse than his bite." With a wave of the paper she was off again, arms swinging purposefully.

Sam was feeling hot and tired when he finally slipped into the water. As he waded in, Amanda launched a perfect dive into the pool. Sam watched admiringly—and with a little envy. He was more of a belly flopper himself. Amanda surfaced beside him. "Hey, Truck."

The others were making too much noise to notice. Still, it was a start. Sam wondered if he could get Amanda to call him that when Ms. Broom was nearby. Then he leaped after a flying beach ball.

A few moments later he stopped to catch his breath.

"My wife would have loved to see this." Cornell Leamish was watching the fun from the pool deck.

"How come she can't?" Sam asked.

"She passed away last year," Cornell Leamish said.

"Oh," Sam said. He felt tongue-tied and foolish. "Sorry."

"No, no," Cornell Leamish waved his hand. "How would you know?"

He stooped to intercept the straying beach ball.

Sam shivered. It seemed odd to be cool already, especially when the water was warm. He looked to see if the sun had slipped behind a cloud. Instead, he saw for the first time that the pool was blanketed by the shadow of the red maple tree at the edge of the lawn. He also noticed a new set of survey stakes. They put the tree on Cornell Leamish's property.

"You see my problem," Cornell Leamish said.

Sam nodded and his teeth chattered. "Is it always like this?"

"For the nicest part of the day. If I hadn't been in Arizona when they put in the pool, it wouldn't have happened." Cornell Leamish shook his head in disgust.

"So what will you do?" Sam asked.

"Cut down the tree, of course."

Sam's surprise was engulfed by the splash from Darryl's cannonball.

It wasn't long before his whole life felt engulfed in the shadow of the tree.

On Thursday, J. Earl was out washing his car, or pretending to. Even from up the street Sam could see he was really keeping an eye on Cornell Leamish. Cornell Leamish was showing another man the tree and his swimming pool.

Sam had been expecting a blast about the paper, but J. Earl beamed at him impishly as he walked up. "No glasses, Foster. See if my letter's in there." Sam obediently opened J. Earl's *Eternal* to the middle page and found the letters to the editor. As he read aloud, J. Earl began to recite along with him:

> "Can anybody out there tell me why the big-city types who move here have to 'improve' everything? First they stick Olympic-size pools into lawns where kids used to run through a sprinkler, and then they find those big trees they adored will interfere with their poolside tans. So, since we all know tans are more important than trees, I have a suggestion: Let's cut them all down, *even if they're on someone else's property,* and put up satellite TV dishes instead. After all, they're modern, they're ugly, and they'll help you see me more clearly on your TV, complaining about it! Signed, J. Earl Goodenough."

"You mean you want to cut the tree down, too?" said Sam. For a moment he was more curious than scared.

"Of course not!" J. Earl glared, "I was being ironic."

"What does ir —"

"Look it up," said J. Earl. "The point is, that tree is a hundred years old. It's history, Foster! Plus all that nature stuff, too."

"How are you going to save it?" Sam asked.

"The power of the press!" cackled J. Earl. He took the paper and began wiping his windshield with it. "Make sure Leamish gets his copy! Oh, and tell your sister to come next Wednesday. Four o'clock sharp."

4
Goodenough for You

On the day of the interview Sam eased his bicycle onto the Albert Street hill. A lot had happened in one week, most of it bad. Robin, who had been fretting about interviewing J. Earl, had not taken it well when Sam had finally revealed the great man was on his paper route. Even though he hadn't mentioned any trouble Robin had yelled, "Sam, you mess up and I'll buy your stupid hockey sweater for Marlon!" Somehow she hadn't yet noticed that Sam was becoming new and improved.

"It would be against the law," Sam had shot back. "He's too pimply to wear it. So be nice to me or I'll mess up on purpose."

That had sounded brave, but really he'd been scared ever since. The Truck sweater was a key part of becoming a new Sam Foster. A mental image of Marlon's orange head, complete with nose ring, poking out of *his* sweater, kept interrupting his daydreams of impressing Ms. Broom. It didn't make hunting for the mystery spot for J. Earl's paper any easier, either.

Then, to make matters worse, he had somehow angered Cornell Leamish. The day after J. Earl's letter appeared, Sam had stuck J. Earl's paper in a bush and then stopped in the shade of the maple, thinking about another swim. It was a warm day and Sam couldn't help noticing a beach ball and an air mattress floating lazily in the pool. They were in shadow, too. Sam had looked up into the stately old tree. High above his head the purple leaves had made a canopy that stretched out over street and lawn alike. As trees went, Sam had had to admit, it was a great one. He'd looked across the lawn. It was a great pool, too—except for the shadow. Which was more important, tree or pool? How could you tell? Sam had frowned and shaken his head. Before he could return to his own concerns, he'd been interrupted.

"Don't say a word to me about that tree." Sam had turned to see Cornell Leamish standing on his verandah, looking far from his usual genial self. "Thanks to your paper, half the town has been after me about that tree. I wish I'd never set eyes on it, or the pool, either, for that matter. But I built that pool for my grandkids, and it's not going to be spoiled. The tree goes. It's on my property, and it's nobody's business but mine. Understand?"

Cornell Leamish had taken his paper and banged the screen door shut behind him. Sam was left speechless. Now, it seemed to Sam that in a movie it would have been nice old Cornell Leamish who wanted to save the tree and jerky old J. Earl who wanted to cut it down. But a cranky Cornell Leamish—well, that spoiled everything. Grownups so rarely acted the way they were supposed to. Sam decided to avoid both men altogether. His Leafs sweater was depending on it.

Which was why Sam had been riding ever since, pitching folded-up *Eternal*s from his bike like the last rider for the pony express. Today however, this was trickier. Wednesday papers were heavy with grocery ads, and the extra weight in his carrier bag made Sam a little wobbly on his wheels. The throwing was harder, too, so it took him longer to get around his route, what with fetching some of the papers out of bushes. After the Doberman mansion though, there was a six-house gap downhill to Number 18, J. Earl's place. As Sam started to roll, he saw some interesting things.

The first was a teenager aiming a video camera at the house. The camera hid his face, but Sam recognized the orange hair and Sonic Vomit T-shirt. It was Marlon. The second was Robin, standing at J. Earl's door, talking into a microphone.

The third was a ladder leaning against the maple tree. A man was high in the branches, tying them with ropes. The fourth was Cornell Leamish, watching from behind the gate to his pool. And the fifth was a truck parked in the Leamish driveway, marked A-1 TREE SERVICE. As Sam began to pick up speed, a second man appeared with another ladder and a chain saw. Oh-oh, thought Sam. Where was J. Earl?

Sam stood up on his pedals for a better look. The weight in his carrier bag shifted to one side, and he wobbled alarmingly. Oh-oh, Sam thought again. That was when J. Earl turned his car onto Albert Street, saw the tree service truck, and blasted the horn right behind him.

"Bwahhh!" Sam shouted, and zoomed, out of control, through the flower bed in front of Marlon. Behind him he heard the screech of J. Earl's brakes, the great man shouting, and Robin yelling, "Keep shooting, Marlon!" Then the Goodenough's garden hose caught in his bicycle pedals. There was a tremendous jerk, and Sam had an upside down view of life in general before he landed on his papers. His bike carried on just far enough to bash into the ladder leaning against the tree.

The ladder toppled, the man in the tree jumped, the man with the chain saw swerved into the pool gate, and Cornell Leamish catapulted into his swimming pool. There was a tremendous splash.

The next thing Sam knew, J. Earl Goodenough had charged in front of him, waving his garden hose. "Turn on the water!" he roared. "Keep filming—it's evidence!" The hose sputtered to life, and J. Earl aimed it up into the maple. "Get outta there right now!"

"I can't without the ladder! For crying out loud, buddy, turn off the hose!" begged the man in the tree, who was quite wet by now. He was perched on a limb, secured by a safety harness. Above him a big branch dangled from a rope.

From where he lay sprawled on the lawn, Sam now saw Mrs. Goodenough come striding up the street, a bag of groceries in each hand. She stopped just beyond the arc of the hose and squinted wryly at the scene over the tops of her sunglasses.

"I can hardly wait to hear about this one, Earl." Her voice cut through the chaos with startling clarity. Then she strode into the house.

J. Earl started at the sound of his wife's voice. "Cut the water!" he called to Robin, a little sheepishly, Sam thought. "Where's Leamish?" J. Earl dropped the hose to the ground.

The gate from the pool opened, and Cornell Leamish stepped grimly out. He was even wetter than the tree service man.

"Trying to slip one past me, eh, Leamish?" With Mrs. Goodenough inside, J. Earl had regained his bluster. He fished a paper from his pocket. "Well, I've got an order from the town clerk that nobody touches that tree till town council checks it out. So get these goons out of here, and remember, I'll be watching!"

Cornell Leamish glared first at J. Earl, then at the tree service men, and finally at Sam. He drew himself up with dignity. Or tried to. It was hard to look dignified after falling into your own swimming pool.

"Cancel my subscription," he said, and marched into his house.

J. Earl whooped and clapped Sam on the back. "Good work, Foster. Gutsy, taking a run at them like that. I knew you had it in you." He was practically dancing with glee. "We saved that tree! And we got it all on film! By golly, Foster, we're a couple of smart ones. We're *all* smart ones! C'mon in! Let's do this interview! What are your names? Never forget a name, just my glasses. Hah! Nothing like a good scrap to get the circulation going." He swept Robin and Marlon, still filming, into the house.

Robin was trying to say something, but as usual J. Earl was too excited to listen. The door closed before Sam realized he should have asked the great man where he wanted his paper.

"Rats," Sam said, and tossed it on the porch. Of course, maybe J. Earl wouldn't mind so much now that Sam had helped save the tree.

Crossing the lawn he saw the tap connected to the hose was sitting at a funny angle. He pushed his bike to the street, skirting the big branch the workmen had brought to the ground. As he rode away he saw a spear of sunshine in the shadow on Cornell Leamish's pool.

"So, apart from the very end, it was a good interview," Mr. Foster was saying as he put the lentils on to boil.

"Oh, sure. I mean, it was great up till then," Robin sat at the kitchen table pulling at the hair on the unshaved side of her head. "But then he got *so* mad. And it wasn't my fault or anything. I tried to tell him, didn't I, Sam?"

"Tell what?" asked Sam, who had just that instant come into the kitchen. He'd been at Grandstand Sports trying on his Maple Leafs sweater again. Amanda had seemed impressed by his tree-saving exploits. Just wait till he told Ms. Broom.

"Tell J. Earl Goodenough about the hose."

"What about the hose?" Sam asked cautiously.

"Well, he went down in his basement to get this book and all of a sudden started yelling. The pipe to the outside tap was cracked, and his stupid basement was full of water. He said it was our fault because he'd been having such a good time that he hadn't noticed before. It was gross, so we left. How can you stand him, Sam?" Then Robin giggled. "It was like a swimming pool."

Sam breathed deeply. "Are you buying Marlon my Leafs sweater?"

"Nah," Robin said, "We're getting Dead Loons World Tour shirts."

Sam spun on his heel and headed out for some paper throwing practice. He could tell he was going to need it for some time to come.

5
A New Broom

By the next morning Sam had begun to think of his exploit on J. Earl's lawn as heroic, even if it had been something of an accident. He imagined a headline in the *Eternal:* BOY RISKS LIFE IN DARING RIDE TO SAVE TREE. Now *that* was the new Sam Foster. All he had to do was let people know about him. Modestly, of course.

When he got to school, Sam spotted Ms. Broom in a circle of students by the basketball hoop. It was a perfect opportunity. Sam jogged over; he liked to jog when Ms. Broom might notice.

". . . run that with one foot tied behind my back." Darryl was talking, for once making something sound easy. In Sam's opinion, Darryl was a boy with more freckles than you'd want to have, but Ms. Broom seemed willing to listen to him anyway. Sam found this unfair because Darryl always had a lot to say. He hogged a lot of the at-school chatting time. And at-school time was all there was. Except for that one awful afternoon in the Bulging Bin, Sam had never seen Ms. Broom any place else around town. (This was strange because Hope Springs was so small you saw everyone, whether you wanted to or not.)

"Ms. B, guess what?" Sam interrupted, jogging in place.

"Sam, you look ready for the district cross-country *meet.*" Ms. Broom flashed one of her toothy smiles. "I need runners for the grades five and six *race.*" She had a way of making words at the end of her sentences explode. Sam tended to goosebumps whenever this happened.

"Sure," Sam volunteered as a fresh crop of bumps blossomed, "I'm a great runner!" He could worry about this lie later. Right now he just didn't want Darryl sounding better than him. He rushed on with a new idea before Darryl could interrupt. "And know what, my Uncle Dave could coach us! I bet I could even get J.—"

"Well, thanks, Sam," Ms. Broom cut in, "but I'm the coach. And anyone who wants to can come out to run at *lunchtime today.*"

J. Earl was going to have to wait. Life as Sam Foster—make that Truck Foster, Sports Star—beckoned. "Gonna go?" Sam asked Darryl.

"Automatic," Darryl nodded. "Hey Sam, I bet doing our paper routes is like cross-country. We'll probably clean up at this!"

"Yeah!" Sam breathed. He couldn't help wondering which of them would clean up more. He stole a glance at Darryl. Behind his freckles Darryl was stealing an appraising glance back at Sam.

Right after lunch, fifteen students gathered in the gym. Looking at the assortment of skirts and jeans, boots and shoes, Sam thought he and Darryl looked pretty athletic in their over-sized shorts and T-shirts. Only Amanda looked more ready to run. Sam turned his ball cap backward to go faster. Darryl did the same.

"The race," Ms. Broom said, "will be 2.4 kilometers long. Today, we'll do an easy 1 K around the neighborhood to see what kind of *shape* you're in."

She led them outside, and nearly everyone was off like a shot. For a moment Sam found himself beside Amanda. "Hey, Truck," she said obligingly. *Truck.* Yesss, Sam thought.

Then, "C'mon," Amanda said, "let's burn these suckers."

Sam tried to follow, but something was burning him under his ribs. He wondered if it had been wise to eat lunch right before running; there was an awful lot of sloshing around going on down there. The burning got worse. He slowed down; the others pulled away.

A few moments later Ms. Broom was at Sam's elbow. By now his legs felt as if they were slowly tying themselves in knots. "Start too *fast?*" she asked, gliding so smoothly she hardly seemed to be moving. Sam nodded between gasps, wondering how Ms. Broom could even think about talking. He noticed Ms. Broom's shorts were actually short and made of some lightweight material. His own clothes seemed to be full of bricks.

"Start slow, finish fast," said Ms. Broom. "Stick with me."

Sam gritted his teeth and followed, hoping Ms. Broom couldn't hear the glugging noises coming from his stomach. It turned out to be easier than pushing along on his own. The burning sensation eased. It wasn't long before they caught up to most of the others. Some were walking; some, like Darryl, had stopped completely. "My shoe came undone," he called, bending over his hightops.

Sam, glowing with pride and exertion, wanted to laugh. He also wanted to talk to Ms. Broom. Unfortunately, he was panting too hard to do either.

Amanda had just finished when Sam and Ms. Broom trotted into the school yard. "Way to go, Truck," she called.

"Excellent," Ms. Broom said to Amanda, and then, "Good run, Sam. Way to hang *tough!"*

The shivers Sam got were enough to make him jog his paper route that afternoon. He tossed J. Earl Goodenough's paper on the run, but slowed next door. Running was hot work and the pool tantalizing. Cornell Leamish was placing a green plaster gnome in his garden. He glared. Sam ran on quickly. He'd almost forgotten about the canceled subscription.

When he shone at cross-country, Sam vowed, and his picture got in the *Eternal,* he'd sneak a copy onto the pool deck. Cornell Leamish would be so impressed that he'd renew Sam's swimming privileges *and* his subscription to the paper. Then all his friends would thank him for inviting them swimming again, and Ms. Broom would probably come along. . . . It would be easy as pie.

As soon as he finished his papers, Sam went looking for the Hope Springs Hydro truck. It was time to talk to Uncle Dave. Mrs. Foster called Uncle Dave her baby brother even though he was a grownup with his own apartment over Hank's Variety. Sam understood because it was what Robin called *him,* particularly when she wanted to bug him. More important, Uncle Dave loved to run. With his help Sam figured on running like an Olympic star.

Uncle Dave and his crew were on Brown Street pruning tree branches that had grown too close to the power lines. As Sam drew closer he saw that Uncle Dave's buddy, Smitty, had stopped to talk as well. Smitty had also worked for Hope Springs Hydro until he won the lottery.

Smitty waved from his pickup. Uncle Dave said, "Hey, Sam. Want a ride in the cherry picker?" He was good about things like that.

"No, thanks," Sam said, "but I have to train for cross-country."

"Well, I'm running 10 K tonight; how about you bike along?"

"Cool!" For a moment Sam wondered if he should invite Darryl along, too. He decided against it. Where Ms. Broom was concerned, it was every runner for himself.

The next morning, Sam limped to school early. He was early because he was the new blackboard monitor; he was limping because his legs didn't seem to bend any more. On the way he passed Mrs. Goodenough out for an early morning power walk. Sam noted ruefully that her legs seemed to work just fine.

"Feeling a little *sore?"* Ms. Broom asked when he winced into the classroom. She had on her fetchingly sporty wire-rimmed glasses. "Don't worry, we'll do some stretching today." Sam stifled a groan. He shuffled stiff-legged to the blackboard.

"Hey, Ms. Broom, know J. Earl Goodenough?"

"I know who he is." The bewitching Ms. B was sorting photocopies. "But I don't keep up with much these days, what with school and the long drive."

Since Mr. Foster taught kindergarten at Doberman, Sam knew teachers had schoolwork, too, but, "A long drive?" Sam asked. Nothing in Hope Springs was a long drive.

"I live in *Toronto,* Sam."

"You do?" Sam was stunned. To most Hope Springers, Toronto was only slightly closer than the moon. "Why?"

"That's where I'm *from.* I just got this job, and I haven't had time to think about moving. It's only an hour and a bit each way." Ms. Broom looked up and smiled a particularly toothy smile. Sam's aches and pains vanished.

"Are you ever gonna move here?"

"Oh, probably, if I get to stay at Doberman."

No wonder he never saw Ms. Broom, Sam thought. This meant he was definitely going to have to do all his impressing at school. The cross-country race was going to be extra important, not to mention his Leafs sweater and good blackboard cleaning. Sam reached for the brushes. He did such a thorough job he'd wiped off two messages marked *Please Leave On* by the time the bell rang.

Amanda smiled as she came in. Darryl said, "Ms. Broom, Sam rubbed off the P.L.O. stuff!"

Sam decided to win the race.

6
White Line Blues

On the day of the race Sam got a ride from Smitty, who had promised some teacher friends he'd help out. Avoiding the school bus was a bonus because Sam was nervous about his clothes. On Uncle Dave's advice he was uneasily wearing his mom's nylon gym shorts, and, equally embarrassing, Robin's powder blue runners. It would be worth it if lightweight clothes helped him win the race.

Sam wondered if Smitty would say something about his outfit, but he didn't. This might have been because Sam never stopped talking, but Smitty was fairly lazy about talking anyway. Besides, Sam thought, Smitty's own dismal combo of work pants, T-shirt, and battered golf hat was no barn-burner, either. He also either needed a shave or had a head start on his winter beard.

They drove north to the Hope Springs Conservation Area, a place Sam remembered from a grade three nature hike where he had gotten two soakers. Today however, October sunshine glowed on a forest dappled with orange and gold. The parking lot was crowded. Sam stopped talking long enough to spot white teeth and a purple wind suit. Smitty drove him over.

"Thanks, Smitty," Sam said, "I'll see ya later." He took a last unhappy look at the hot pink stripes on his shorts and hopped out.

Instantly, someone hooted, "Hey Sam, niiiice outfit!"

"It's for running," Sam said cautiously, tugging his T-shirt down.

"It's for girls," someone else said decisively. The boys laughed.

"So what?" said Amanda, "It's a smart idea."

The boys laughed again. Sam felt naked.

"I think so, *too,"* said Ms. Broom. The laughing stopped. Sam looked at her gratefully. She had a new haircut that made her even more breathtaking. Then he looked at Darryl. His friend stood smirking at him in his clunky basketball shoes and shorts like boat sails. Yesterday, Amanda had called Darryl a snail on snowshoes. Definitely right, Sam thought. Automatic. Friend or not, he was going to clean Darryl's clock.

As the starter's pistol sounded for the grades seven and eight race, Ms. Broom pinned number cards to everyone's T-shirts. "We'll jog a bit," she said, "then stretch."

They trotted off, Sam moving easily beside Amanda, but wishing he was talking to Ms. Broom. Lately, she had been telling Sam how well he was doing. She told everybody that, of course, but Sam was sure she told him more.

They passed Smitty, who was helping move picnic tables by the finish line. Ms. Broom pointed out the powdery white line marking the course. "So you don't get *lost,"* she said. Groups from other schools drifted past. Sam began to realize how many runners there truly were. Some of them, he noticed, even had real uniforms. A lot of them looked big, too. And fast. Up until this moment Sam's legs had felt strong enough to bend steel. Now, for a second, they felt as if they might disappear.

They stopped to stretch. More questions began to crowd in on him. What if they ran miles and miles at other schools? What if they trained all year round? He looked at Darryl, freckles bobbing as he did jumping jacks. What if he didn't even beat Darryl? What if Darryl had been training secretly? What if he'd been running slowly to fool everyone? Truck Foster, Olympic star, evaporated. All that was left was a skinny grade sixer in girl's shoes—who needed to go to the bathroom. Darryl joined him. When they got back it was time for the race.

Ms. Broom gathered them round. "Okay, everybody. Remember: start slow, finish fast, follow the white line, and don't look *back*. I'll be cheering for you at the finish." As Sam passed her she patted him on the shoulder. "Good *luck,* Sam." For a moment Sam had the strength of ten.

A hundred or more runners jostled for positions at the starting line. Sam found himself wedged between two boys from another town who looked practically big enough to shave. One of them noticed Sam's shoes. He grinned. The strength of ten sank into a swamp of embarrassment. Sam tugged his T-shirt down over his shorts again.

Then someone pushed in beside him. It was Amanda.

"Those your mom's shorts?" she asked loudly. The boys snickered. Sam nodded. Amanda pointed. She wore the same kind. "I bet she got them at our store."

"I guess," Sam muttered, keeping his head down.

"Hey," Amanda leaned in and whispered, "stick together. We'll win."

Sam stared at her. He felt about as powerful as a broken elastic.

"Runners, take your marks," a voice crackled through a bullhorn. A hush fell and the runners grew very still. "Set . . ." Everyone leaned forward, then *CRACK!* went the starter's pistol, and they were off in a rush.

Sam stumbled across the uneven ground, faster than he wanted to go, but everyone was going fast in the confusion. Amanda, he knew, was somewhere on his right and Darryl on his left. Start slow, finish fast, he reminded himself as everyone plunged down a hill and across a bridge. But what if this *was* slow for everyone else?

Across the bridge the crowd strung out in a line to the bottom of a hill. Two runners panted a few yards ahead. Sam found he passed them without speeding up. He set his sights on the next runners. He passed them as they rounded the hill, then several more as they crossed a picnic area and entered the forest.

The trail wound and twisted through the trees. A teacher at one of the turns called encouragement. Sam knew he was slowly gaining on more runners, but he kept his eyes on the trail to avoid the roots and rocks poking out of the dirt. The white line had almost vanished under the pounding of hundreds of shoes from other races.

As he ran he thought in a jumbled way about hot pink Maple Leafs sweaters, snails with toothy grins, and Darryl and Amanda hopping on snowshoes until it all boiled down into a chant that fit the rhythm of his breathing: "Hop Darmanda's Leaf Teeth, Hop Darmanda's Leaf Teeth."

He passed three, four, five more runners, and now, deep in the forest, there was no one close in front. Sam's legs were beginning to feel as numb as his brain. The trail forked in two. Sam leaned automatically to the right.

Then, out of nowhere, a voice called, *"Sam!"* Sam didn't hear the rest, but he guessed what it meant: Darryl, right behind.

Sam streaked down the path as if Robin herself were after him, pounding hard for a minute or more until his toe caught a root and he stumbled. Don't look back, Ms. Broom had said, but as he slowed down, gasping, Sam peeked over his shoulder anyway. No one was behind. No one was in front, either. He looked down: there was also no white line.

Something inside him lurched alarmingly. Maybe the line had just been trampled out. He jogged a little farther. Nothing. No one. With a growing sense of disaster, Sam sprinted back the way he had come and saw to his horror that the trail branched off in three different directions—with no white line on any of them.

Which one had brought him here? He stopped and gazed wildly around. Somewhere close by, his race was on. Darryl and Amanda were running; Ms. Broom was waiting. Which way to go? He started down one trail; it didn't seem right. He tried another, but couldn't be sure.

Then, from over on his left, Sam thought he heard a voice. Fighting down his panic, he raced for it.

The path went up around a bend and there, perched on a tree stump with his back to Sam, waving his arms dramatically, was a short man with a familiar looking bald head.

"When in disgrace with fortune and men's eyes," he rasped loudly,

"I all alone beweep my outcast state,

And trouble deaf heaven—what the . . . !"

He leaped to his feet as Sam burst out of the trees.

"You!" snapped J. Earl Goodenough. His head was already turning pink. "Whaddya mean, charging in here? Can't I get some privacy in a public park?"

"I lost my race," Sam fumbled. "I mean, I got lost from my race."

"What race?" J. Earl's eyebrows knit furiously.

"My cross-country race," Sam panted desperately. "Have you seen a white line around here?"

"A what line? You know in my day we had a little respect for—"

"A *white* line," Sam almost shouted. "It marks where the race goes."

"A white—so that's what it was for. I thought maybe they were planning to put a highway through. That's not here, Foster. You're off track, way off track."

"I know," Sam pleaded. "Just tell me which way it is!"

"Well, I don't know how you got here, but it's way down at the beginning of this path."

Sam was already running.

"And Foster," J. Earl called, "forget we bumped into each other."

Sam tore along the new trail as fast as he could. Just when he thought he'd never reach the end he saw a powdered white line cross his path.

"Yesss," Sam gasped, and then he groaned as he realized J. Earl's trail had taken him back almost to the beginning of the woods. Sam turned to his right and ran like he'd never run before.

It wasn't until he got to the far side of the woods that he caught a few straggling runners. Legs aching and lungs bursting with the effort, he passed them. He churned up a short hill and there, across the field, was the finish line. Another familiar figure in floppy shorts and basketball hightops was just struggling across.

By the time Sam finished, no one was paying much attention any more. This was fine with him; he felt closer to crying than at any time since his first day of kindergarten.

"Sam, what *happened?"* Ms. Broom cried. "Amanda said you got *lost."*

"I yelled to you when you took the wrong turn," Amanda said, "but you didn't listen."

Sam started. "You? But—"

Darryl silently offered him some Gatorade.

"I thought—" Sam began, but then he stopped and looked guiltily at Darryl. How could he explain? It would only sound mean and dumb. His big chance to impress Ms. Broom was gone anyway. Instead, he lifted the Gatorade. "Did you win?" he asked Amanda between big gulps.

"Third," she said. "I'm going to get a medal. Too bad you didn't hear me, Sam."

Sam was too tired to answer. He handed the bottle back to Darryl and said, "Thanks. Wanta help with each other's papers this aft?"

"Automatic," Darryl said.

It was quiet on the ride home. Finally, Sam said, "Hey Smitty, what does 'When in this place with fortunate men's ties' mean?"

"'When in disgrace with fortune and men's eyes,'" Smitty corrected. "It means, 'When everybody thinks I'm a goof.' It's Shakespeare."

"What?" Sam said. "How do you know?"

"I had to memorize it in grade ten. Old Mrs. Goldenrod

made us recite in class. Embarrassing or what, eh? It's been stuck in my head ever since." And Smitty began to recite:

"When in disgrace with fortune and men's eyes
I all alone beweep my outcast state . . ."

The words were like music, even the way Smitty recited. Sam didn't know what most of them meant, but a poem about feeling dumb did seem to fit the bill right now.

He closed his eyes. Not everyone thought he was dumb, even if he had gotten lost. Ms. Broom might not be rushing up to marry him, but she felt pretty sorry for him. That was something. Amanda had thought he could keep up with her, and she had come third. Darryl was still his friend. He would have come fifth last if it weren't for Sam.

And then there was J. Earl. J. Earl often did think he was dumb, but now the great man looked pretty dumb himself, spouting mushy poems in the woods. Maybe that would make him stop griping about where to put the paper. Sam vowed to remind him if it didn't.

And soon, Sam would have his Leafs sweater. He burped a gentle Gatoradish burp and began to feel better.

"That then I scorn to change my state with kings," Smitty finished.

Change with kings? Sam thought that was pretty dim. He'd trade with kings any time—after he showed his Leafs sweater to Ms. Broom.

7
Cold Comfort

The mild autumn weather finally vanished in a cold snap. Cornell Leamish drained his pool. Around town the leaves on the trees seemed to change color instantly, as if they'd just remembered they had to and were hurrying to catch up. Soon Sam was kicking through soggy piles of them as he did his papers. Then they were gone, and the bare days of November gave way to an early snow that left adults dreaming of Florida and kids dreaming of blizzards.

The snow melted, of course, but not before Darryl concocted plans for a snowball storage system that would take advantage of basement freezers all over town.

"We all save our sandwich bags from school," he explained to Sam, "and every time it snows, everybody in the gang makes five snowballs and stores them in their freezer."

"What gang?" Sam interrupted.

"The gang we'll make. I haven't decided what to call it yet. The important part is that every snowball has to go in a separate bag so they don't stick together. I did some tests, and sandwich bags are best 'cause you can seal 'em up easy and—"

"How about 'The Secret Blizzards'?" Sam interrupted again.

"Huh?"

"For the name for our club."

"I dunno, I'll have to think about it. It's complicated, you know? Anyway, you gotta make sure to squeeze all the air out when you seal 'em up, and you gotta take 'em out exactly . . ."

The explanation went on for several more minutes. Fortunately, Darryl had some bubble gum to share in the meantime.

Unfortunately, it didn't snow again until January, and everyone forgot to save their lunch bags. Sam was vaguely disappointed. Being involved in a secret snowball club had seemed like something that might revive his efforts to become special. His report card had been unspectacular, and there were no more races to run or trees to save. He'd finally gotten his hockey sweater at Christmas, with a little help from his parents. Unfortunately, three other kids had received jerseys as well. Ms. Broom said that some days the class looked like the Leafs bench. With all that competition, no one but Amanda ever remembered to call him Truck, no matter how much Sam hinted about it.

Of course, there was always a chance he might turn out to be a foundling child. Perhaps as a baby he'd been accidentally left behind by billionaire parents whose limousine had broken down in Hope Springs. If he was, though, no one had ever thought to mention it. Sam was beginning to suspect he was doomed to dullness forever, or at least until spring.

Spring this year meant in-line skates. Sam had realized he needed a pair ($119.95 plus tax) as soon as he put on his Truck sweater. Amanda naturally had some, and Darryl wanted them, too, for roller hockey next spring. Sam also had plans: imagine Ms. Broom's pleasure when he could blade along with her on her daily jog.

The desire for skates kept Sam slogging around his paper route on cheek-freezing afternoons, but by February, with no end to winter in sight and less than half the money he needed in his bank account, he was close to fed up. His whole life seemed to be about waiting for one thing or another: enough money, enough snow for tobogganing, enough just plain growing up.

Of course, Sam wasn't the only person feeling this way. By midwinter, workaday adults in Hope Springs were wishing for things as well: namely, the money for a vacation down south. This naturally reminded them of rent, mortgages, car payments, and heating bills, which made them remember how cold it was all over again. Which sooner or later led everyone to think of Smitty. Smitty, of course, was famous in town for winning a bundle in the lottery. Word was he'd spent most of it, but no one knew for sure. He did lots of handyman work for friends, but no one could remember him doing much for pay. In fact, the only things Smitty ever did for sure were sleep late, grow his winter beard, and stroll down to Hank's Variety every Friday to buy a few more lottery tickets.

Hope Springers noticed everything everyone did, so they noticed this, and soon Hank was selling a lot more tickets than usual. Robin had to write a story about it for *The Hope Springs Eternal,* where she was now a co-op student. After she interviewed Hank, she fibbed about her age and bought a couple of tickets herself, being in need of funds for the upcoming Aggressive Microwaves concert in Toronto. On her way out she met her father, who had been sent to take a little gamble on behalf of the Hope Springs Band Shell Restoration Committee. Amanda's mom was right behind. Hank said he was considering a revolving door.

Sam didn't go to Hank's; kids couldn't buy tickets. Instead, he formed a partnership with Darryl. If he was going to be rich, he thought, he might as well have a friend who was rich, too. It seemed more fun that way. Together, they went to someone who lived right above the store.

They found Uncle Dave in the parking lot at Hope Springs Hydro. Sam stood, shoulder cocked and hands on hips, trying to look like a working man as they talked.

"Are you sure you can afford this?" Uncle Dave asked.

"Sure we're sure," Sam was indignant. "We've got paper routes."

"And I've got a system," Darryl confided. "It's really—"

"Tell him later," Sam said. It was too cold to listen to one of Darryl's explanations. Forgetting to look like a working man, he pulled his hands back inside his elastic cuffs and hopped from one foot to the other on the freezing pavement.

"Well, then, what do you guys need a million dollars for?"

Sam liked to talk about many things, but romantic in-line skating with Ms. Broom was not one of them. "I didn't say we needed a million. Anyway, we'd all split it. Are we partners or what?"

Uncle Dave frowned at his ancient car. It looked as if the trunk was about to fall off. "Why not," he sighed. "I'm buying tickets anyway. But tell me any time you want to quit."

"Automatic," Darryl said. They each dug ten dollars of paper route savings out of their pockets.

"Remember," Sam said, handing over the cash, "it's a secret." How grown up could you get?

Uncle Dave didn't need much reminding about secrecy: everyone knew Mrs. Foster frowned on lotteries—even though she'd bought some tickets on behalf of the Hope Springs Food Bank. "The food bank is not a vacation," she said flatly, explaining the difference. "Besides, Smitty's win was a fluke, and *he* is a bit of a flake. I mean, I like him," she added, "but sometimes he's just a big kid." Mrs. Foster was organizing a bingo night for the food bank at the time and was not in a cheery mood. Bingos were a lot of work.

In-line skates were not a vacation, either, Sam thought. They would give him and Darryl a better chance of playing in the NHL when they grew up—if they decided to do that instead of being astronauts. Still, he made sure not to breathe a word of his lottery playing to either of his parents. There was no point upsetting his mom now. They could find out *after* he won.

And then there was Ms. Broom. Being even a partial millionaire would certainly make Sam special in her class. Of course, it would make Darryl special, too. Sam dismissed this thought. Ms. Broom might listen to his over-freckled friend, but Sam was certain this was pure politeness; there were some things a teacher just had to do. In the crunch Ms. Broom would know who was who.

Two weeks later, nobody but Hank was any richer. Sam was getting tired of waiting again. He was a little worried, too, although he didn't tell anybody that part. Nonetheless, Smitty's annual Serious Fishing Winter Weekend came just in time. Mr. Foster announced it one night as he packed up his euphonium to go to a practice of the Hope Springs Society Stompers, a Dixieland band he played in as a hobby. Perhaps because he felt grown up playing the lottery, or perhaps just because he was wishing so hard for a change, Sam surprised even himself by announcing, "I want to go, too."

Mr. Foster snapped his horn case shut and gave his son a quizzical look. "Sam, it's just a bunch of grownups sitting around ice fishing and playing cards. You'll be bored stiff."

"No, I won't," Sam insisted. "I like that stuff now. I'm older."

"You didn't seem too thrilled when we went fishing last summer."

"That was different. Now I'm more mature."

Robin snorted behind her copy of *On the Road.* Sam glared at her.

"I don't know that I'd call Serious Fishing with the boys 'mature,'" Mrs. Foster put in. Mr. Foster glared at *her.* She smiled back and went on, "But it's the same weekend as bingo. I could use the quiet."

Mr. Foster shrugged. "Well, it's fine by me. I'll check with Smitty, and if there's not too many going, you can come along."

"Yesss!" Wait till he told everybody at school! Sam did a small victory dance across the kitchen that ended when his sock skidded and he bonked his head on the refrigerator.

"How mature," said his sister.

8
A Hot Ticket

As it happened, only Smitty, Uncle Dave, and Mr. Foster were free on the chosen weekend. Sam and his dad were bundled up and ready Friday afternoon when Smitty and Uncle Dave arrived in a borrowed pickup truck with an extended cab. Sam was so excited he didn't even care too much that his dad had insisted he wear snow pants. Everyone considered snow pants babyish after grade four.

Still, it was reassuring to see Uncle Dave had his snowmobile suit on. Smitty, too, looked even bigger than usual with his wild winter beard and a lumpy red parka. It was the old down-filled kind that got all puffy in the cold until the person wearing it looked like the Michelin tire man. He'd replaced his golf hat with a black and gold Boston Bruins toque for the winter. Hats were important to Smitty; he was thick in the middle, but a little thin on top.

Sam and his uncle climbed into the jump seats in back, Mr. Foster popped a Creedence Clearwater Revival tape into the cassette deck and they were off. Here he was, Sam marveled, one of the guys. He felt taller already. As they rode north up Highway 28, Sam leaned close to Uncle Dave, man to man over the five gallon water drum. "Did you get tickets for tomorrow?" he whispered.

Uncle Dave gave a thumbs-up. "Got four."

"Same system?"

"No, phone numbers this time." Sam nodded and settled

back. Phone numbers sounded good. They made as much sense as combining birthdays and license plate numbers, an idea so complicated it could only have been Darryl's. This change was going to bring them luck—Sam could feel it. He needed all the luck he could get.

It was long after dark when they got to Smitty's cabin. Smitty eased the truck over the icy ruts of the lane and parked by the back door. Sam stepped out. The night air was like an electric shock. "Well," said Uncle Dave, flipping up his hood, "no mosquitoes."

It felt even colder inside. Summer smells of lake water, bacon grease, and wood smoke still lingered faintly in the frigid air. Sam looked around at the battered furniture, the wood stove, the ancient refrigerator, the moldy chunks of indoor-outdoor carpet, and sighed with pleasure. It was perfect.

Everyone had a job to do. Sam lugged in sleeping bags, Uncle Dave the supplies. Smitty and Mr. Foster got to work on the wood stove. As the fire began to crackle, Smitty said, "Time to check on the fishing hut."

"Wait up," Sam called, anxious not to miss anything. "I'll come, too." Who knew what adventures might be waiting?

They stepped out into a night that felt almost like daytime. The snow glowed like blue neon. Sam looked up through the bare branches of the trees and saw the moon suspended in a clear, frozen sky. Silence rang all around them. Sam's ears began to sting.

Smitty led the way out onto the frozen lake, snow squeaking under their boots. The ice rumbled ominously beneath their feet. Sam felt a little stab of alarm.

"Don't worry," Smitty said, stamping on the surface for Sam's benefit. "It's just settling. Always does that."

Sam tried to keep the nervousness out of his voice. "Boy," he said, "if it was summer I guess we'd be swimming pretty hard."

"Or sitting in the boat," said Smitty, who was not prone to panic.

The ice fishing hut looked something like the outhouse behind the cabin: a tall plywood box with a slanted roof and a stovepipe. Snow was packed around the bottom. Smitty went in and rattled the lid on the oil heater. "Looks good," he said.

They turned and stood looking back to the lights of the cabin. All around them the mysterious blue light glowed from the drifted snow. "This is like exploring the South Pole or something," Sam blurted.

"Uh-huh," said Smitty. "I sure hope Dave bought barbecue chips."

They started back. Sam made himself stroll as slowly as Smitty. It seemed a good time for confidences. If his hunch about being lucky was right, he had to find out some things right away.

"Hey, Smitty, what happens when you win the lottery?"

"Well, you've gotta take the ticket to this office in Toronto," Smitty said. Sam saw he'd need a ride.

"Then you get your check and they take your picture for the paper." He decided to wear his Leafs sweater for sure. "And there's people there to give advice about the money."

No problem there, Sam thought. In-line skates and no more paper route. He asked, "But does everybody go nuts and everything?"

"Nah," Smitty said, "I went fishing. Everybody's different, I guess. I got to quit my job, do some traveling, buy a coupla things, but I was happy before, too."

"Well, like, did you race out and tell anybody?"

"I told the guys at fishing. They didn't believe me."

Sam got closer to the point. "Didja tell any girls?"

Smitty shrugged inside his parka, which had swollen up so much in the cold that it looked as if it might float away with him. "I told my mom."

"Smitty!" Sam said in exasperation

"I wasn't going out with anybody right then." He looked at Sam and grinned. "Got somebody you'd like to tell?"

"Smitty!"

Serious Fishing turned out to be mainly about playing cards, eating junk food, and sleeping late, so it was well after lunch when everyone finally got their lines in the water. The rules were that if you caught enough to eat for dinner, you had to quit. On the other hand, if you didn't catch anything, you had to stay out until suppertime.

Sam didn't want to admit it, but Mr. Foster had been right: after the first half-hour, ice fishing was incredibly boring, especially if you were waiting for the lottery draw at five o'clock. Sam started fidgeting around two, bobbing so impatiently his dad asked him several times if he needed to use the outhouse. He didn't, but he went a couple of times anyway, just for something to do.

"I'm sure getting hungry," Sam said hopefully when he came back the last time.

"Have some more chips," Smitty said, patiently jigging his line.

Sam looked at Uncle Dave for help. He seemed to be asleep.

Finally, at six o'clock, Smitty stood up and stretched. "Let's go. All this fishing is getting in the way of cards." They packed up the gear, shut off the heater, and headed in, Sam leading.

Now everyone was starving. Sam and Mr. Foster pried frozen burgers apart for Uncle Dave at the wood stove. Smitty broke out some of his disposable knives, forks, and plates. He'd bought a lifetime supply when he won the lottery. Sam took the burgers to Uncle Dave. "The lottery!" he hissed. They could already be zillionaires and not even know it.

"Hey, Smits," Uncle Dave called, "can you get CKHS? They give the lottery wins at the end of the news."

Sam stopped moving. After feeling lucky all weekend, all he felt now was a knot in his stomach and a dry mouth. He had to win this time. Smitty flicked on the radio. "Geez, forgot to get tickets," he said, as the weather forecast ended with ". . . and no chance of snow until much later in the week."

Uncle Dave was stirring the fire as the announcer began

reading the winning numbers. He relinquished the poker and fumbled for his wallet. As the numbers were repeated he began to look excited. "I think I got some of those, Sam." He shuffled hastily through the tickets. "Just a sec—wait. . . ."

Sam's heart started to pound. "Yesss!" Uncle Dave yelled, "Three numbers! We won five hundred bucks!" He whooped and flourished a ticket in the air.

Sam felt a rocket take off inside him. "We won!" he shouted. "I knew it. We won!"

"What do you mean, 'we'?" Mr. Foster asked from across the cabin.

Sam was too excited to answer. "What numbers? Lemme see." He grabbed for the slip of paper. Then, "Ow!" he cried, and snatched his hand back from the open stove—as Uncle Dave let go of the ticket.

The slip of paper fluttered in the warm draft from below, then did a graceful little flip and swooped through the hole in the wood stove.

"Get it!" cried Uncle Dave.

It was too late. With a tiny *poof* the ticket burst into flames.

Five hundred dollars crumbled to ashes before their eyes.

9
You Know What I Got?

Sam was still feeling rotten when Smitty dropped them off at home Sunday afternoon. Having to explain his secret lottery scheme to his father hadn't made him feel any better. When they got in the house, Sam dropped his sleeping bag. "What smells different?" he complained. He wasn't in the mood for any more changes.

"Cigarette smoke," Mrs. Foster answered. She was ironing in the kitchen. She nodded toward another basket of laundry. "I'm just about to wash my last night's clothes. There's always a million smokers at a bingo. It was like breathing mud. Speaking of which," she sniffed, cocking an eyebrow at Sam, "have you been smoking cigars?"

"No-oh. They were."

"Just one," Mr. Foster said. "It's the rules. How much did you make at bingo?"

"Just over a thousand dollars." Mr. Foster whistled. "And boy, did we work for it. People playing twenty cards at once don't put up with any mistakes from dummies like yours truly."

Mrs. Foster spread another shirt on the ironing board. Mr. Foster poured himself a coffee, then scratched his unshaven chin. "You don't seem very thrilled about making a thousand bucks," he said. "It sounds pretty good to me."

Mrs. Foster shook her head. "It's not that. It's more—well, there were people there playing who probably need to use the food bank. I don't mean they shouldn't be at bingo—everybody needs some fun. I just mean it seemed we were making money for our charity from the people who could least afford to give it. That's not the way it should be. It was sad."

Sam wasn't in the mood to listen. He stumped up the stairs. Mr. Foster nodded at his son's retreating figure. "Somebody else has been doing a little gambling, too."

"What are you talking about?" asked Mrs. Foster.

Sam groaned and stumped faster, so he wouldn't have to hear his dad's retelling of the lottery disaster.

As he reached the top of the stairs, the telephone rang. Sam picked up the phone in his parents' room.

"Hey," Darryl's voice squawked, "did we win anything?"

Sam stared at his thermal socks. "Well, kinda. But not exactly."

"Huh?"

Sam took a deep breath. "Well, we had a ticket for five hundred dollars, but it burned up."

"What?" Darryl sounded as if he'd just laid an egg. "How?"

"Well, see, like, me and my uncle—aw, never mind how, it just did, okay? And I'll get you your money back for the ticket."

This last rash promise was out of his mouth before Sam even knew he'd thought it.

"It's still a rip-off," Darryl complained.

Sam didn't feel like arguing. After he hung up the phone he went to his room and flopped on his bed. A little while later he heard a knock. His mother came in and sat down beside him. "You must be a pretty disappointed guy," she said. "What did you want all the money for?"

"I dunno. In-lines, I guess." Sam stared at the ceiling.

"But honey, you've got a paper route. We worked it out, remember? You'll have enough by spring break."

Sam shrugged. "The lottery was faster."

"Sweetie, it's the middle of winter. You won't even be able to use in-line skates till spring."

Sam didn't answer. His mom gave him a long look.

"Now listen, Sam. Kids aren't allowed to buy lottery tickets. It's against the law. I called Uncle Dave and asked him not to do this with you any more. He agreed. He said you'd only shared a few tickets, but that's not the point. He can afford it; you can't. It's a hard lesson, but maybe it's a good one, and if you want to make the money back, I can find a couple of hours for you to work at the Bin this week." She patted his hand and rose to leave. "So don't despair. You don't need the food bank yet."

As the door closed behind her, Sam let out a sigh he'd been saving up for a long time. A couple of hours at the Bin wasn't going to help. Nobody but him knew it, but the ticket they'd lost had used up the last of his paper route savings. All the money he'd earned—tramping through slush, folding papers with cold fingers, missing tobogganing—was gone. When his parents found out, the explosion would make crashing on in-line skates seem like bouncing on marshmallows.

By next morning, snow was whispering down. The gray sky and silent flakes wrapped the town like a muffler.

"You don't have to pay me for the ticket," Darryl announced on the way to school. "My aunt came over for dinner last night and gave me twenty dollars because she forgot my birthday. Now we can buy extra this week."

"We're not allowed to any more," Sam said, ducking into his stand-up coat collar. "I don't have any money left anyway."

"Nothing?" Darryl's freckles seemed to swell with amazement. "Wow, that's too bad," he said cheerfully and shuffled off to jump in the snowdrifts by the school parking lot. Darryl's snow boots were the only things clunkier than his hightops.

The snow kept on falling as Sam floundered around his paper route after school. The survey stakes on Goodenough's lawn had been reduced to tiny bumps under a blanket of white. The Goodenoughs were away; Sam didn't have to leave a paper. A note saying WRONG AGAIN, FOSTER was pinned to the front door anyway in case Sam forgot.

As he finished his papers he saw Smitty's pickup rolling slowly up the street. A snowplough blade was attached to the front. Sam's gloom deepened.

Smitty put down the window. "You done?" he called. "Give you a lift." Sam climbed in and crumpled his carrier bag on his lap. The cab was nicely warm.

"We've got us some snow," Smitty said. "I'll be ploughing tonight. I'll tell ya, I'm ready for spring."

"I'm not," said Sam. He watched the wipers scoot a few soggy flakes across the windshield. For all he cared now, it could keep snowing till July.

They crossed the south bridge over the river and passed the town park. The Doberman Memorial Band Shell loomed up in the middle like half a giant igloo. Smitty said, "You were counting on winning some lottery money, huh? Bought a lot of tickets?" He waved to someone going by. "Gets pricey."

"Uh-huh" Sam nodded, looking away. He could feel his face getting hot. Smitty pulled over to the curb.

"Well, it just so happens that I won a little on Saturday. Here." He reached inside his parka, then tossed an envelope onto Sam's lap. "Two hundred and fifty bucks. What you should've won. But you've gotta promise: no more tickets if you need money. You play stupid stuff like that for fun. If you really care about it, you're in trouble. Got it?"

Sam nodded. His brain seemed to have gone numb.

"Promise?"

Sam nodded again. "But don't you need—I mean, everybody says—"

Smitty laughed. "I know what everybody says. I'm doing okay. I had a whole lot more money, and you know what I got?"

"What?"

"Bored," said Smitty. "Now, get outta here. I gotta run."

"But I'm not home yet," Sam said, still too stunned to think straight. Two hundred and fifty dollars!

"I thought you might want to go into the Grandstand," Smitty nodded across the street. "In-line skates?"

Sam stumbled out of the truck in a daze. As the pickup turned at the Four Corners he yelled, *"Thanks, Smitty!"* because he'd forgotten to before. He looked inside the envelope: twelve twenty-dollar bills and a ten. He hopped up and down. He wanted to tell somebody. He wanted to shout. He wanted his skates.

Amanda was sorting her sports cards and doing math homework when Sam came bursting into the Grandstand.

"Hey, Truck," she grinned. It occurred to Sam how nice it was of Amanda to call him by this name when no one else ever did.

"You don't have to call me that, you know," he said.

"I know." She shrugged. "It's okay, I like to." Her face was pink, but then it was hot in the store.

"Oh. Well, thanks," Sam said. "Hey, where are the in-line skates?"

"Oh, that's spring stuff," said Amanda, "We won't have them in again until March. Hey, are you getting in-lines? Fantastic. We can play hockey this spring."

"For sure."

Now that he had the money, Sam found waiting for skates would be no problem at all. With all the snow nobody would be blading for a long time. He said good-bye to Amanda and started home. Cars were creeping in the storm. Sam hopped over piles of slush, feeling as if he could stride over mountains. Maybe school would be canceled. "No chance of snow. . . ." he remembered the radio from Saturday night. He laughed out loud. Fat chance of snow was more like it. And then he remembered Smitty saying something as the radio blared, and he stopped grinning and his mountain striding slowed and he stopped.

If Smitty hadn't . . . He pulled the envelope out of his pocket and looked inside again. All that money. A snowflake landed on one of the twenties. The wrong place for snow. Or was it the wrong place for money? His thoughts swirled.

What would Smitty do? Smitty didn't care about money at

all. But he wasn't Smitty. What would Smitty want *him* to do? He gazed at a snowcapped parking meter, then at the river, blanketed in white, then back along the street, past the Grandstand to a darkened storefront. He stared for a long time, and then he knew. He took out enough money to make up his and Darryl's lost paper route earnings, then sealed the envelope.

Back at the Grandstand Amanda lent him a pen. He printed "From G. Smithers" on the envelope, then headed down the street to the dark storefront. He slipped the envelope through the letter slot. The food bank volunteers would find it when they came in tomorrow morning. Then he brushed the snow off his knees and headed home. The mountains he had just been striding over seemed to be gone. He didn't think he felt like an adult, and he didn't feel like a kid. Whatever he was, it felt right.

10
The Bulging Binnacle

"So," puffed Ms. Broom, "What's this Hope Springs a Leak Race?"

"It's excellent," Sam panted back. He had unexpectedly encountered Ms. Broom jogging as he did his papers. Now he was blading shakily along beside her, on brand new in-line skates, just the way he'd dreamed. It had taken a lot of hard saving, plus his share of what he'd kept from Smitty's gift, but as of yesterday he had his skates. Sam went on about the race, made eloquent by the muddy scent of spring.

"They race down the river, canoes and stuff first, but the *best* part is the Crazy Craft. There was one last year like a space ship and this other one with a big plastic gorilla and palm trees. And they sink and stuff and everyone gets soaked and it's freezing. It's *great.*" Sometimes it was hard not to talk like Ms. B. "And know what? My dad was in it one year with some teachers. Their boat fell apart, and it took them four hours, and some one dropped water balloons on them at the end. Dad said he was cold for the next three years."

"Sounds like *fun,*" said Ms. Broom. "I'll try to catch it."

"Really?" Sam enthused, "You'll *be* here?"

"Uh-huh. I'll have things to do. But right now, I've got to turn at this street. *Bye,* Sam!"

"Well, come to the race for *sure,*" Sam called after her. Then his tongue bladed ahead of his brain. "'Cause *I'm* going to be in it."

With that he rumbled onto Albert Street and into a typically large Hope Springs pothole. *"Ayyyiiii . . ."* Sam's arms windmilled frantically, and he bailed out into the ditch. It wasn't elegant, but neither was the paving in Hope Springs.

Sam clambered back up and wiped off the mud. At least he was pretty good at landing on his newspaper bag, he thought. He looked down the long slope of Albert Street and shuddered. Maybe it was better to have stopped here before he got really rolling. As he picked his way cautiously across the gravel it occurred to him he was now facing another problem as well: Ms. Broom was expecting to see him in the Leak race.

This meant he would have to enter, and this, Sam knew, could be tricky. Kids were only allowed in the river race with adults; you had to build your own Crazy Craft *and* you had to pay an entrance fee. On the other hand, it would certainly be a nifty way to stand out in a world full of lottery losers, Leaf sweaters, and in-line skates. He pondered all this as he made his way cautiously down the hill, past Doberman's and along to J. Earl Goodenough's.

Sam tossed the paper at the porch. The WRONG AGAIN, FOSTER note still clung, weather-beaten, to the door even though the Goodenoughs were back. On the lawn the red maple tree was budding. Now that the ground had thawed, the stakes around the tree slumped at all kinds of crazy angles; the town still hadn't decided who the tree belonged to. Hope Springs, as Mr. Foster put it, was a town that had to hurry up just to be slow.

Sam clung to the tree to rest up for a moment, still thinking about the race. Over by the Leamish pool he noticed some new green plaster gnomes had been added to the still-bare garden. They'd look good on a Crazy Craft, Sam thought. He wondered how heavy they were.

This wasn't helping. He forced his mind back to the problem of entering the race. Who could he get to help? Smitty had already helped with the lottery money. Uncle Dave was busy working overtime for a new car. His dad always said he wouldn't enter the race again if you paid him. Sam thought harder. His dad's words had stirred a memory. The night before, Mrs. Foster had been complaining about the price of advertising in *The Hope Springs Eternal.* Robin, still a co-op student there, had defended the paper—until Mrs. Foster said she might have to cut Robin's pay at the store to afford her ads. Sam fired off his last papers and wobbled off for the Bulging Bin.

He managed the rolling hop up onto the sidewalk as he passed the Grandstand and the swerve around the litter basket outside the Cuppa Cafe. In control for once, he leaned back gently to brake as the door opened at the Bulging Bin just ahead. It wasn't enough. In a moment of panic Sam realized he was going to flatten whoever stepped out. *"Look out,"* he cried, and pulled back hard. There was more windmilling and the usual follow-up. Too late, he remembered there were no papers to cushion his fall.

The person leaving the store was Marlon, with, as usual, his video camera running. Marlon rarely talked himself, but Robin said he wanted to make rock videos. Now she looked out behind him. "I can hardly wait to see the replay."

"People with orange buzz cuts can't watch replays," Sam said, from his seat on the sidewalk.

Robin smiled. "Know what? If you're wearing that helmet to protect your brain, it's in the wrong place." The door swung shut.

Climbing back to his feet, Sam saw a poster for the race in the front window of the Bin. Inside, Mrs. Foster was at the cash, and Robin had returned to cleaning the cooler at the back. Sam waited until Mrs. Winkler bought her weekly supply of licorice allsorts, then said, "Hey, Mom, guess what? I've got a great idea for free advertising for the store!"

Mrs. Foster put her hands in the pockets of her long white apron. "Fire away," she said.

"Well, everybody will be watching the Leak race, right?" Sam gripped the counter to keep from rolling around. "So we should enter a Bulging Bin boat with a big sign on it about the specials and everything. Then everyone would come and shop here."

"That's the dumbest thing I ever heard," Robin called from the back, but to Sam's delight, Mrs. Foster actually seemed to be thinking about it.

"Sam," she said, "I think you've got something there."

"We could use those big plastic barrels you've got at the back for floaters," Sam said excitedly.

His mom nodded. "We'll need help."

"Dad said no already."

"That's okay," Mrs. Foster said. "We'll start with Robin."

There was a screech from the cooler. "Not in a million years!"

Mrs. Foster just smiled. She called to Robin, "Who won the canoeing medal at camp four years running?"

"Moth–er!" Robin shrieked, "That was when I was *twelve!"*

"And who has promised me they would do more than listen to alternative bands?" Mrs. Foster kept smiling.

"MOTH–ER!" Two shoppers entered the store and stopped when they heard Robin. Mrs. Foster smiled at them, too, as Robin marched to the cash. "Mother, that race is, like, totally dorky!"

"Who owes her mother a big favor for a loan and a Saturday off so she could go to Toronto with her friends?"

"MOTTTHHH–ERRRRRR!" Sam hadn't seen Robin this upset since he'd drawn fangs on her Undeniable Saucepans poster. "I'll never be able to show my face around town again."

"Lucky for us," Sam observed, wheeling around. Robin would have swatted him if his skates hadn't shot out from under him on their own. Looking down at him, she said, "You'll pay for this, Sam."

It didn't take Mrs. Foster long to get things organized. By that night she had Sam filling out the entry form, Robin rounding up life jackets, and Smitty and Uncle Dave collecting floatable junk to make a Crazy Craft for five. It had turned out that they owed Mrs. Foster a couple of favors, too. Sam was beginning to see why she was good at running her own business.

By the next evening they were all gathered in the chill of Smitty's big double garage, lashing blue plastic forty gallon barrels together, end to end. Mrs. Foster was supervising, and Robin was grumpily lettering the words BULGING BINNACLE . . . NATURALLY on a bed sheet that was going to fly overhead.

"What is a binnacle, anyway?" Sam asked, holding tight to a rope.

"Who cares," Robin muttered.

"It's where the compass is on a ship," Smitty explained. He took the rope. "Hey, Sam, remind me to ask you about something afterward."

Sam nodded and stepped back to see how the Crazy Craft was shaping up. It looked like five blue barrels end to end. "Know what? We should get Marlon to video us, first building, then—"

"Forget it," Robin said. "Marlon's not going to know."

"What? How are you gonna keep it a secret?"

"None of your business, nerd-brain, but if you tell, I'll print it in the paper that you wear Cookie Monster jammies and your sweetie, Ms. Broomball, will read it."

Sam gasped. *"I do not.* She *is not* my—" He choked on "sweetie."

Robin offered a sinister smile. "Melissa Sweeney told me you and her dumb brother Darryl have got the love contest of the century over her. So keep your mouth shut, or you're dead."

"I need more hands here, Sam," Mrs. Foster called.

Dazed, Sam turned back to the barrels.

"Say," his mom said, "why don't you get Darryl to help us out, too?"

"I'll tell you why—" Robin began smugly.

Sam whirled and glared at her. "I'll ask him tomorrow," he said confidently.

Really, Robin had him worried. Not that there was anything to that love contest of the century stuff, he told himself. For one thing, no matter what Sam thought about his teacher sometimes, he still got impossibly squirmy over words like *love* or *sweetie* or *smooching.* The way Sam put it, he just wanted Ms. Broom to think he was *special.* And besides that, Sam knew Darryl couldn't possibly think Ms. Broom liked *him.*

But if Robin embarrassed him in the paper, his chances of becoming Truck Foster, Somebody, would be zero. He'd be a joke, and Sam had had enough of that when he'd thrown his underwear at J. Earl Goodenough. He had to show Robin she was wrong.

Sam saw his chance the next day, as everyone chose up sides for ball hockey. He said, "Hey, Darryl, guess what? I'm gonna be in the Leak race. Wanna be in our boat?"

"Nah," Darryl said casually, "I'm already in one."

Sam was stunned. "You're in the race?"

"You kiddin'?" Darryl said, just before disappearing behind a grape gum bubble. The bubble popped. "We're gonna win." He picked a stray shred of purple off his freckles. "Ms. Broom's gonna be there, too."

"Hey, you guys, get over here." Amanda, one of the ball hockey captains, was circling on her in-lines, sizing up the players.

Sam swallowed hard as they skated over. Darryl couldn't really think . . . *could* he? Could *she?* Could Robin be right? Of course not, Sam told himself, but he was furious anyway. Getting into the Leak race had been his idea, and he felt as if Darryl had stolen it. Well, he'd take care of Darryl. He stopped. "Like fun you'll win."

"Oh yeah? I'll bet you hockey cards."

"Automatic," Sam said fiercely. His chest swelled heroically beneath his Leafs sweater. Ms. Broom's honor was at stake.

"Bet traders?" Darryl offered.

"Nope," Sam said recklessly. "Everything. The whole set."

Darryl blanched a little under his freckles. "Everything?"

"Unless you're chicken. Hey, Amanda," Sam called, "you'll be there, right?"

"Yup." Amanda was flipping a dime to see who got to pick first.

"So you hold our hockey cards, okay?"

"Winner gets them all?" Amanda called back, picking up the dime. She'd won.

"Yup." Sam nodded.

She stuffed the dime into her jeans. "See you at the finish," she said. "Okay. I pick Sam."

11

Hope Springs a Leak

The morning of the race was chilly and damp. Smitty and Uncle Dave loaded the Bulging Binnacle into the back of Smitty's pickup truck, where it stuck out the open tailgate. If it wasn't a masterpiece, Sam figured, at least it wouldn't sink. This was important if he was going to beat Darryl.

Everyone else piled into the Foster car for the trip up the river to the starting line. Sam shared the back seat with Uncle Dave's girlfriend, Lorraine, and a bearded stranger in a toque and lumberjack shirt.

"Is the glue on your beard waterproof?" he asked Robin.

"It's not glue—it hooks around my ears."

"Well, no one would know it was you."

"Good. Just keep it that way. Call me Vince."

The starting point was several miles north of town. Down the road, lined with parked cars, Sam could hear the Hope Springs Society Stompers, his dad among them, wonking away. People were milling around in costumes and life jackets and wet suits, carrying paddles and odd pieces of equipment.

The river itself was brown with the spring runoff. A few big chunks of ice remained on the banks. Standing beside one of these, with his back to the water, was J. Earl Goodenough. Sam hadn't seen him since before the great man had gone away. Today J. Earl looked a little different. His bald head was covered by a green and orange Hope Springs a Leak souvenir cap, its brim shaped like a duck's bill. J. Earl had a microphone pinned on, and he was talking into a TV camera a few feet away. Sam couldn't resist waving into the camera.

"Joke's on you, Foster," J. Earl grunted. "Camera's not on yet."

"Well, I was just practicing, too," Sam said boldly, carried away by the excitement of the day.

Smitty and Uncle Dave carried the Bulging Binnacle behind J. Earl to where the Crazy Crafters were waiting to get into the water. The barrels now had thick pieces of Styrofoam attached to their sides like the running boards on an old-fashioned car. Sam had painted some beach balls gray, and Uncle Dave had put them at the ends of the Styrofoam pieces so they looked like sets of giant barbells.

Hockey stick handles rose skyward to hold the banner. Mrs. Foster began to tie it on. Sam got busy taping on BULK UP AT THE BULGING BIN signs. As he finished, Robin came trudging down from the car with paddles, life jackets, and the white aprons they were all supposed to wear. She kept as far from the camera as possible.

Out on the water, the canoe and kayak part of the race was about to begin. Being faster, the paddlers always went before the Crazy Craft. Sam saw that behind her beard Robin was watching Lyle Doberman bob in what looked like a brand-new kayak.

Robin and her female friends often referred to Lyle, who was in grade twelve, as a "hunk." Hunk of cheese, maybe, Sam thought. To boys he was just one of those jerks who snapped his towel at you in the pool change room. "Bet he's got as many zits as Marlon," Sam said. Robin, or Vince, didn't answer.

Sam finished buckling his life jacket over his apron and turned to look for Darryl. Instead, he saw J. Earl again, standing by himself as his cameraman fiddled with something. Too excited to stand still, Sam went over to ask him about the paper.

"Hey Mr. Goodenough, where do you want—"

The great man turned. "What is it, Foster, can't you see I'm working?"

"Oh, sorry," Sam said, "I thought you were just standing here."

"I am. That's when I'm working."

"I thought you were working when you were talking on TV," Sam said.

"That's the easy part. The real work is thinking it up first, figuring how to make it sound natural."

"It sounds really natural on TV," Sam assured him. "It doesn't sound like you think at all."

J. Earl's bushy eyebrows gathered like storm clouds beneath the duckbill of his cap.

"I mean—" Sam said

"I know what you mean," J. Earl said grumpily. "But you've gotta start thinkin' before ya gab, Foster, that's my advice." He flicked a glance from side to side, then lowered his voice. "Speaking of which, have you ever mentioned to anybody about that time I was, uh—"

"That time you were saying poetry?"

"Keep it down," J. Earl winced. "Yes, then."

"No," Sam said truthfully, "you told me not to."

J. Earl looked hard at him. Then he smiled. "Thank you."

"CRAZY CRAFT CONTESTANTS!" crackled a loudspeaker, *"IN THE WATER NOW, PLEASE!"*

"I gotta go," Sam said, then stopped. "Hey, Mr. Goodenough? How come you *were,* uh, you know, saying—"

"Put it this way, Foster. What you do isn't always what you are. Now get going or you'll miss this idiotic race." J. Earl turned back to the camera, pulling the cap down tighter on his shiny dome. Sam ran for the Bulging Binnacle.

The others were waiting. Smitty and Uncle Dave, the only crew members with wet suits, waded into the swirling water and held the Bulging Binnacle steady while Robin, Sam, and Mrs. Foster climbed aboard. "Sam, pull your splash pants over your boots," Mrs. Foster ordered. Straddling a barrel like this was difficult to do: the life jacket kept his arms puffed out awkwardly. How was he going to paddle?

Sam sat up and held on to the ropes as Smitty and Uncle Dave pulled them out farther into the river. He could feel the chill rising beneath him. Even with the Styrofoam the Bulging Binnacle was a lot tippier than he had imagined. To calm down, he imagined Ms. Broom fainting and falling in the river as they won the race. He'd dive in and save her. Then they'd get married.

The Binnacle now floated at the edge of the first row. Uncle Dave held them steady at the stern, Smitty at the bow beside Sam. They waited for the start.

"Hey," Smitty said, "I've been meaning to ask you. Did you—"

"Look," Sam interrupted, "there's Darryl!"

Next to them was a Batmobile boat, then a pirate raft with its crew in masks and costumes, and a sea serpent. And there, beside the serpent, was Darryl. He was perched on something labeled the Sweeney Steamer, which seemed to consist mainly of giant inner tubes with a phony smokestack and paddle wheel. Sam shook his head in disgust.

"EVERYBODY READY," blared the loudspeaker. Sam gripped his paddle. Another race against Darryl, he thought, but this time he'd win. Darryl would see how dumb he had been. Over the rushing of the water, Sam could hear J. Earl blathering into the camera.

"GET SET . . ." Smitty and Uncle Dave tensed to push for the middle of the river, where the current was fastest. Sam braced his feet, and for the first time noticed that a rubbery gray wire was caught on the Bulging Binnacle. He reached for it.

"GO!" A cheer went up. The Batmobile folded neatly in two and sank. Smitty and Uncle Dave pushed, Robin dug in with her paddle, and Sam, still reaching, almost fell off his barrel. A second later there was a shout of surprise from the riverbank and a splash. Then J. Earl Goodenough surfaced beside them in a tangle of rubbery gray wire from his disconnected microphone.

12
Think or Swim

"Ahhgggh! Help, it's freezing! Get me outta this!" J. Earl roared. Smitty reached with one hand and grabbed him. "Help me to the bank!" J. Earl howled, then looked at the cameraman. "Never mind," he roared at Smitty. "Get me on the durn boat!"

Smitty pushed. J. Earl scrambled up and flopped, dripping and hatless, in front of Sam as the current finally swirled them into the middle of the river. Smitty and Uncle Dave squeezed on as well. The pirate raft was out ahead of them, the Sweeney Steamer, now sporting the sea serpent's tail, just behind.

"Are you okay there, Mr. Goodenough?" Sam's mom asked.

"I've got whiplash and I'm freezing," J. Earl groused, "but it was a great camera shot, so if we win I'll be fine." That was when the first splash hit them.

Everyone shrieked; it was like a blanket of ice. By the time Sam could breathe again, the Bulging Binnacle was bouncing over the first shallow rapids. "Hang on, there's more," Uncle Dave shouted. The Binnacle rocked and twisted and scraped the bottom. A gray beach ball broke loose and floated away.

"This is my first marriage all over again," groaned J. Earl. Sam was too busy to wonder what he meant.

An hour and a half later, when they were three quarters of the way down the river, the sun came out. People on the river-bank cheered. Sam would have cheered, too, if his teeth hadn't been chattering so hard. His rubber boots had filled with freezing water an hour and fourteen splashes back, and he couldn't quite feel the paddle with his fingers. He could feel his rear end though. An hour of bouncing over rocks on a blue plastic barrel had had a tenderizing effect.

Nobody else on board looked any happier. Robin and Uncle Dave were still struggling to keep them pointed in the right direction while Smitty tried to steer them around the rocks. Robin's beard was slowly disintegrating. Sam didn't think he should mention it yet.

Otherwise, the Bulging Binnacle was holding up pretty well. And, Sam reminded himself, except for the pirate raft somewhere up ahead, no one had passed them. In this twisty-turny part of the river, not far from the end, no one else was even in sight. He might be cold and he might be wet, but he'd be just fine when Ms. Broom and the rest of Hope Springs saw him beat Darryl.

They bounced off a rock and swept sideways around the next bend. On the breeze came a snatch of Dixieland music. "We're almost there," Sam cried, and they ran aground on a rock. Behind them the Sweeney Steamer hove into view. Its smokestack was bent crazily in the middle, and there was something wrong with the paddle wheel, but it was floating just fine.

"Hurry!" Sam shouted, as Smitty and Uncle Dave got off to push.

"Hurry is right!" chipped in J. Earl. His blue lips made an interesting contrast with the rest of his head, which was quite pink. "My public isn't going to want me coming second to a bunch of inner tubes. Make it snappy, Foster. You got me into this!"

There was no time to argue. Sam clambered off and started to push, too. J. Earl rocked forward like a rider on a stubborn mule. Robin and Mrs. Foster leaned hard against their paddles. The Bulging Binnacle floated free as the Steamer went bouncing by. Darryl's sister, Melissa, waved. Darryl stuck out his tongue.

Sam flung himself back aboard. "Paddle," he shouted. "Paddle hard!"

"Put a cork in it, Sam," Robin sighed. "I am, like, totally drenched and this is totally dorky. Who cares if they beat us?"

Think before you gab, J. Earl had said. Sam only had one thought, and he hoped it was a good one: "You don't want Melissa Sweeney to beat you in front of Lyle Doberman, do you?"

"Paddle," cried Robin. "Paddle hard!"

Everyone leaned into their work but J. Earl, who, not having a paddle, just leaned. The Steamer was wider than the Bulging Binnacle, and it ran aground on the rocks at the last bend. By the time it broke free, the Bulging Binnacle had pulled alongside. They were neck and neck going into the last long stretch of brownish-white water through the center of town to the park.

The crowd was thick now along the riverbank, and above the shouts and clapping Sam could hear the Stompers tooting and thumping down in the band shell. Somewhere out there Ms. Broom was watching.

"Watch out!" yelled Uncle Dave. They rumbled over some shallow rapids as if they were sliding down a flight of stairs. There was a sudden drop. Sam's stomach met his ears, then there was a tremendous splash, and the two craft were swirling together.

"Out of the way," J. Earl roared, "Sunday drivers!" But it was too late; Smitty and Uncle Dave were laughing too hard to paddle, and Robin was struggling with her soggy toque, which had slipped down over her eyes. This had kept her from noticing her beard had fallen off in the last big splash. By the time she could see again, the Sweeney Steamer and the Bulging Binnacle were hopelessly tangled. Just to be safe, Mr. Sweeney grabbed a hockey stick, and Mrs. Foster grabbed what was left of the Steamer's paddle wheel.

They drifted to the finish line, J. Earl suddenly waving and jaunty in case his cameraman was filming. As they passed under the bridge someone dropped a water balloon on him. Looking up, Sam could have sworn he saw Cornell Leamish.

All together they steered for shore. People helped them drag the two craft up onto the riverbank. "Whaddya mean the camera wasn't working?" Sam heard J. Earl barking. "I coulda died out there!"

Sam felt a pinprick of disappointment. So much for being on TV. As he looked around, the feeling grew sharper. Ms. Broom was nowhere in sight.

Darryl was craning his neck, too. Sam felt a stab of suspicion. Before he could ask who Darryl was looking for, Darryl said, "Rats, a tie for second."

"Second?" Sam exclaimed. He had forgotten about the pirate raft. Sure enough, it was farther down the riverbank. He groaned. "I guess nobody wins."

"I guess," said Darryl, pouring water from a rubber boot only slightly larger than his usual shoes. "Anyway, Amanda's not here with the cards."

"Maybe she's up there," Sam said. Something was going on up on the bridge. "Or maybe it's Ms. Broom," said Darryl. They hurried up to investigate.

It was Marlon. His head was jammed between the struts of the bridge railing. People were trying to get him out.

"What happened?" Sam asked.

"He was leaning out filming," the man next to them said, "and I guess something surprised him because he sorta jumped and his head got stuck."

"Hey, Marlon," Sam called, "want me to hold your camera?"

Marlon managed to nod and he passed the video camera back.

Sam held it up and peered through the viewfinder. The camera was hard to hold steady because his teeth were racketing like a typewriter, but as he swept it over the chilly, sunlit scene in the park, Sam saw his dad stomping off a tune, the natural foods snack stand, J. Earl wrapped in a blanket and barking at his cameraman again, and Robin glowering beardlessly as Melissa Sweeney chattered to Lyle Doberman.

"Rawb–inn," Sam yelled, "Better come up here!" He put the camera to his eye again and this time saw Amanda. She was standing beside the pirate raft. Her black mask was off, and she was swinging two bags that might have held hockey cards. She waved.

Sam gulped. "Oh no," said Darryl. They went down to meet her.

"We won," said Amanda, now wearing a Toronto Maple Leafs sweater. Sam noticed it had the same number as his.

"I know," he said.

"If that twerp Doberman hadn't been hot-dogging around in his kayak at the finish line we would have set a new record, too. Hey, like my sweater?" Sam nodded.

"Are you gonna keep our cards?" Darryl asked.

"Nah," Amanda said, "I've got them all anyway. Here. I've got to go over to the trophy stand." She paused. "Want to come, Sam?"

Before he could answer, someone called, "That was *fantastic!*"

It was Ms. Broom.

13

A Friendly Move

She was with two older grownups. "Meet my mom and dad," Ms. Broom said.

"Great *finish!"* Mr. Broom enthused. Obviously, it ran in the family.

"I bet you're all glad it was so close," said Ms. Broom, missing the point entirely. To her parents she added, "These three are such good friends, always doing things together."

Darryl shifted uncomfortably while Amanda colored and glanced at Sam; Sam changed the subject. "How come you're here today, anyway?"

Ms. Broom gave them a toothy, conspiratorial grin. Sam would have gotten goosebumps if he hadn't already had them.

"I've been arranging to rent an apartment," Ms. Broom said. "I'm teaching here again next year, so I'm moving to town next *week."*

"Where?" Sam blurted, hoping it would be on his paper route, even as a new idea bubbled up. "Hey, my friend Smitty has a truck. He'll help!" Which really meant Sam would help. The only kid in class who helped: it put goosebumps on top of goosebumps.

"No, wait," Darryl cried, "we've got a *big* truck."

Sam gritted his teeth. Amanda rolled her eyes.

Ms. Broom laughed. "Thanks, but I'm all set. My family's helping." She turned to her parents. "What did I tell you?

Everyone is so *friendly.*" Ms. Broom and her parents moved off with a wave.

Friendly, Sam thought. That was it! It would be his best chance ever. Still, he'd need help. He stole a glance at Darryl. Could Robin have been right about a contest? Soggy and shivering under his freckles, Darryl looked harmless enough. Besides, his dad worked at Homestead Hardware, and that could come in handy for what Sam had in mind. So, for that matter, could the Grandstand. Sam took a deep breath.

"You guys," he said, "I've got this idea."

It took until Monday to get everyone organized, but it was really quite easy. There were, after all, a lot of kids who liked Ms. Broom. Jessica's mom managed the Weclips Hair Stylon, Ian's mom worked in the bank, Holly's parents owned the Cuppa Cafe, and Mrs. Foster, of course, had the Bulging Bin.

The only person who didn't want to help was Amanda.

"But why?" Sam pleaded in the school yard. "Don't you like her?"

"She's okay," Amanda shrugged. "How come *you* like her so much?"

"I dunno," Sam fumbled. He thought about toothy grins, sports watches, jogging, exploding words. None of them quite explained what it was that gave him goosebumps, and he wasn't going to mention those. "I just do. Everybody does."

"Not enough to turn the town upside down for her," Amanda sniffed. "I'd rather go blading. Want to come with me after school?" Her face was pink. Sam guessed she'd been running.

"I can't," he said. "Stuff to do for Saturday."

Amanda's face flushed darker, but she didn't say anything. Instead, she proceeded to clean Sam's clock at wall ball.

Even without Amanda, Sam soon had just about everything in town covered, from vitamin pills to cable TV. Darryl made a list of it all when everyone met Wednesday after school. Sam said, "So anyway, next Saturday, wherever she goes we tell them who she is and make sure it's extra friendly, right?"

"Right," said everybody. Sam headed off to deliver his papers before Darryl could make it sound more complicated than it was. Ms. Broom was sure to find out such a terrific plan had been his idea. And then . . . well, it was worth thinking about.

Saturday morning Sam tied on his big apron and helped Robin fill containers in the Bulging Bin. Knowing his plan was about to unfold made it hard to concentrate. He spilled marmalade on Robin's head. Robin screeched and raced for the sink.

"It's not *that* bad," Sam offered. "You already have orange hair."

"Then go stick your head in the peanut butter, bozo," Robin squawked from under the tap. She'd been touchy since her beard had fallen off in the Leak race.

"Hey," Sam protested, "what you do isn't always what you are."

He still wasn't sure he knew what J. Earl had meant by this cryptic pronouncement. Still, it seemed to fit the occasion.

Robin snorted in disgust. Sam went to clean the front window. He waved to Mrs. Goodenough as she came power-walking by. Darryl panted up not long after. Ms. Broom and family were heading for the Cuppa Cafe. Sam whisked off his apron.

The Cuppa Cafe was filling up with the usual Saturday crowd by the time the boys got there. The others were waiting at the back counter. "They stopped at the grocery," Jessica said. "I got my cousin Steffi to meet them at the door."

"And my dad is going to give them free coffee and Ms. Broom a free lunch," added Holly. "Look, here they are! Dad! Dad!"

Ms. Broom and her family squeezed around a table up front, and Holly's dad appeared beside them, as if by magic, with mugs and a coffee pot. Sam saw surprised smiles, then they were all laughing. "Awesome," said Darryl, making a check mark on his list.

As they ate, Darryl read off the names of people still waiting to be friendly to Ms. Broom. It was impressive. "Let's go say hi," Jessica giggled when they finished. "Then the flowers."

Sam jumped up. This would be the perfect time for Ms. Broom to find out all this friendliness was his idea. Still, he couldn't just go bragging: Think first, J. Earl had said. The best thing would be to get someone else to mention it. "Boy," he hinted to Holly, "I hope Ms. Broom doesn't find out whose idea this was."

"For sure," said Holly. Sam wasn't sure if she got it or not.

Ms. Broom saw them and waved them over. Instantly, Darryl asked, "Is everybody being friendly?"

Ms. Broom smiled. "And *how!*"

Sam tried to look modest but important at the same time. He also tried to keep from screaming, "It was my idea!" at the top of his lungs. It was all so much of a struggle that, before he knew it, he'd missed his chance.

Next door at the flower shop they all chipped in. When Ms. Broom left the cafe, Mrs. Vandervennen, the florist, was waiting with the flowers. "Welcome to Hope Springs," she said, "from some friends of yours." Ms. Broom gasped.

As they peeked out from behind the potted plants, Jessica sighed, "She must think this is the friendliest place in the world."

"Automatic," Sam agreed, thinking, thanks to me.

"Thanks to us," Darryl said. Sam saw he had a problem.

14
The Friendliest Place in the World

Luckily, the others turned out to be no better at hinting than Sam was. They all asked Ms. Broom how the friendliness was, of course. Jessica brought in coupons from the drugstore, Holly a church bulletin, Ian a map of town. Darryl dug up a screwdriver, but then what could you expect, thought Sam, when Mr. Sweeney worked at the hardware? The best Sam could do was leftover *Eternals* and a bag of bulk trail mix—until he heard his parents had invited Ms. Broom for Saturday dinner.

It was the perfect chance to give Ms. Broom a hint, uninterrupted by other kids. The only problem was, Sam was having a pizza and video games marathon with Uncle Dave and Smitty that night, over at Uncle Dave's apartment.

"I have a lot of homework. Maybe I should do it and go after dinner," Sam suggested to his mom.

"Now I've heard everything," said Mrs. Foster. "You do homework on a Saturday? Uh-uh, buster. You're at Dave's and Robin is going out with Marlon. It's dinner for adults. Ms. Broom can manage a day without you." All Sam could do was call Smitty and ask him to pick him up later than they'd planned.

When the doorbell rang on Saturday, Sam leaped down the stairs. Ms. Broom stood on the porch, wearing jeans and carrying a couple of packages. Sam thought she looked even nicer away from school.

"Hi!" he practically bellowed. "Is everyone still being

friendly?" Before Ms. Broom could answer, his mom and dad appeared, shooed Sam upstairs, and steered Ms. Broom to the kitchen.

Sam slipped back to the front hall anyway, listening for a chance to take credit for making Hope Springs the friendliest place in the world. At first the conversation was promising. Then Ms. Broom said, "To be honest, everyone's *so* friendly I feel a little *weird*. Just today, the cable TV man knew my classroom, someone I'd never met asked if my mom's headaches were better, and the bank teller liked my new curtains. I haven't even *made* them yet! It turned out her sister sold me the material."

Ms. Broom laughed a little, but she didn't sound happy. "I dress up to buy a newspaper so the whole town won't think I'm sloppy. It's like being on display somewhere. Is it always like *this?"* Her "this" exploded like popcorn.

Sam caught his breath. This wasn't part of the plan. His mom said, "Well, I grew up here. Everyone knows your business, but there's not many that are mean about it. We have to get along, after all. Right now you're a new face. Things will settle down."

"I hope so," Ms. Broom sighed. "Maybe I'm more private than I thought. I'm beginning to see that one of the nice things about the city is not knowing *everyone."*

"Lots of teachers make sure not to live where their schools are," said Mr. Foster. "But, hey, look on the bright side. When I started here twenty years ago the principal told me I wasn't allowed to buy wine in town. And look what you've brought us." A cork squeaked out of a bottle. "Progress!"

Everyone laughed but Sam. The last thing in the world he wanted Ms. Broom to know about now was his friendliness plan. If somebody blabbed, she'd be mad at him forever. He'd have to tell the others and do something, fast. After all, he thought, it was *their* plan, too.

There was a knock on the side door. Then Sam heard Smitty's voice. "Sam!" his mom called.

"Nancy Broom," his dad was saying, "this is Glenn Smithers, better known as Smitty." Smitty and Ms. Broom were shaking hands as Sam stepped into the kitchen. Smitty's winter beard was gone, but his T-shirt and crumpled golf hat had returned with spring.

"Let's go, Smitty," Sam said, trying not to look at Ms. Broom, but as usual, Smitty was in no hurry. He lifted an arm to scratch his back, a move that hoisted his T-shirt a little too far off his stomach.

"So," Smitty said, "teacher, eh? Livin' here now? Where ya from?"

To Sam these were just the kind of nosy questions Ms. Broom had been complaining about. He wanted to hide in the fridge. It was all he could do to keep from grabbing Smitty by the waistband of his work pants and dragging him out the door.

"She's your teacher, huh?" said Smitty as they finally climbed into his pickup truck. "Did I see her back at cross-country?"

"Yeah, yeah," Sam said, "let's go." He kicked at an empty pop tin Smitty had left on the floor. Smitty laughed. "What's the hurry? We were having a nice chat in there."

Sam rolled his eyes. "Geez, Smitty! Right before you got there, she was complaining about how everyone in town is so nosy and how it's bugging her."

"She didn't look bugged to me. You look bugged."

"I'm not bugged," Sam snapped.

"Well, let me know when she's not so bugged," said Smitty, putting the truck into gear. "I'll ask some more questions. Which reminds me. I wanted to ask you about something, but now I forget what."

Monday morning Sam told the others the bad news.

"Boy, are you in trouble now," said Holly.

"And how," said Ian. "I don't know how you talked us into it."

"I always thought it was a dumb idea," Darryl said, and tore his list into little shreds.

"What?" Sam shouted. "But you helped! You—"

"It was your idea and you did all the phoning and you bossed us all," Darryl explained calmly. "It's your fault."

He began to shuffle away. The others followed.

Sam called, "But we don't have to . . . Darryl . . . you guys! Wait!"

Nobody did. Darryl called back, "Don't worry, we won't tell."

There was something meanly happy in his voice that Sam had never heard before, and all at once he understood something: love or otherwise, there really *was* a contest of the century.

For a moment he was unable to move. How could Darryl possibly think . . . ? Couldn't he see that Ms. Broom liked . . . ? Sam's astonishment was replaced by a darker question: how could *he* have been so wrong? And if he'd been wrong about that, what if Ms. Broom liked Darryl—freckles, hightops, and all?

Sam turned and stumbled across the playground. It was as if he'd reached the top of the climbers only to have them dissolve into thin air. What could he do? The worst part was that he really had figured out the friendliness problem, too. He kicked clumsily at nothing and froze, struck by a lightning flash of inspiration: *He could do it all himself.* And who would Ms. Broom thank? Who would Ms. Broom really *like?* Sam "Truck" Foster, that's who, not a certain traitor ex-best friend. Darryl was history. Darryl was toast; toast with major freckles. Let it be the contest of the century; the Truckster was ready. Sam squared his shoulders defiantly and marched into school.

15
Famous Last Words

All Hope Springers knew that if you said the right things in the right places at the right times around town, a lot of talking would get done for you. Sam got started right after his papers were done. By Thursday, he figured, the problem would be solved.

Thursdays were always busy in the Foster household. Mr. Foster stayed late at school, Robin had a co-op day at the *Eternal,* Sam had his papers, and Mrs. Foster had to bustle home after closing the store because it was her night to make dinner. Mrs. Foster never enjoyed making dinner—she said being around ingredients all day took away her appetite—so she always made spaghetti. No one complained. Spaghetti was safe, and that was important in a household where your father might cook Broccoli Noodle Surprise.

This Thursday, however, Mrs. Foster's mind was not on pasta when she got in from the Bulging Bin. "Sam!" Her voice carried from the front hall even louder than it had the time she'd found socks in the dishwasher. Sam, who had been watching TV and listening to his stomach rumble, sat bolt upright on the couch.

Before he could move any farther, his mother loomed over him. She said, "Mrs. Vandervennen told me today that she heard from the meter reader who heard at the Cuppa that Ms. Broom is being harassed and wants everybody to leave her alone before she goes crazy. Do you know anything about this?"

"Um . . ." Sam said, and found he couldn't talk.

"I'm asking," Mrs. Foster went on, "because the word at the bank is that Ms. Broom asked a kid in her class to tell people to get off her back because she was too close to a nervous breakdown to do it herself and that she was having to go to the city for treatment. And I thought of you because Mrs. Vandervennen says you and some others were a regular welcoming committee a couple of weeks ago. I think you have some explaining to do, mister."

"So do I," said Robin, who had just come in. "This sounds good enough to put in the paper."

"What's good enough?" asked Mr. Foster, stepping in behind her.

Mrs. Foster explained again. Mr. Foster stopped smiling. He said, "Nancy was telling me today that now everyone around town is treating her as if she has the plague. The people that do talk ask if she's feeling any better. She can't figure it out."

Sam sighed. He had that feeling again—that the climbers were disappearing, and it looked like a long way to the ground. He took a shuddery breath and told what had happened, more or less.

"Talk about going overboard!" whistled Robin. Sam glared at her, but his parents seemed to soften a little. "Well, dear, your intentions were good," said Mrs. Foster, "and maybe Ms. Broom overreacted, but what in the world did you say to everyone?"

Sam looked at the ceiling. "I just said I'd heard she wanted to be private because she was used to the city, and everybody being so friendly made her nervous."

Robin gasped. "Don't you see how rude that sounds, Sam?"

"No," Sam complained. "Everyone else just got it mixed up."

"Well, that's what happens when people gossip, isn't it?" sighed Mr. Foster. "People don't think before they talk."

Sam looked up. Robin said, "I'll say."

Mrs. Foster ignored her. "So what are you going to do now, Sam?"

"Say I'm sorry, I guess."

"Yes, but how are we going to make things easier for Ms. Broom? The whole town is wondering about her."

Sam had a vision of himself explaining to the whole town. It would certainly make him special. Even so, he said, "I don't know."

"Well, you'd better think of something fast."

After supper that night Sam biked along with Uncle Dave on his ten kilometer run. Track and field was coming up at school. Sam wasn't sure that would matter now, but riding and worrying was better than sitting at home and worrying.

Halfway along they turned onto a street Sam knew all too well.

"That's J. Earl Goodenough's house," Sam pointed downhill. "He's always griping that I leave the paper in the wrong place." Indeed, J. Earl had complained to Sam twice since the Leak race.

"So why not leave it in the right one?" Uncle Dave wiped his brow.

"Because I don't know where it is."

"So ask him."

"I do," Sam complained, "but he never listens."

Uncle Dave shrugged. "There's gotta be a place you haven't tried."

"There isn't," Sam insisted. "It's totally unfair. And he never makes sense. Like, see that tree? It wrecks the guy next door's pool, and J. Earl Badenough won't let him cut it down. So he writes this showoff letter to the paper, and he says, 'Power of the press, Foster!' But he never even reads the paper. What a jerk!"

It felt good to blame someone else for something. Sam's complaining gathered momentum as his bike rolled down the hill.

"And the pool guy is a jerk, too. He says we can go swimming, then gets mad at me just 'cause the stupid letter is in the paper. It's not my fault. I'm just the paper boy!" All at once Sam was swept by genuine anger. It seemed as if everything he had tried all year had gone wrong. Fairness had deserted the world. How could he hope to be special when a mean-spirited combination of J. Earl Leamishes and Cornell Goodenoughs had taken over?

"So they had it surveyed?" Uncle Dave nodded at the orange stakes as they drew level with the house.

"Yeah, yeah, way last fall," Sam fumed.

"Well, they're in for a surprise," Uncle Dave said. "That tree isn't theirs. It's on town land."

Sam was barely listening. An idea had just sprouted like an orange survey stake in the middle of his misery.

"Hey, wait up!" Uncle Dave called, but Sam was already gone.

16
True Confessions

It cost Sam ten extra unpaid shifts at the Bulging Bin, but Robin finally agreed to do it. For Ms. Broom, she said; not for Sam.

The next morning Sam went to school early with Mr. Foster. They found Ms. Broom putting a new display up on the bulletin board.

"Sam has something to say to you," Mr. Foster said, then went out, closing the door.

Ms. Broom put down her stapler and looked at Sam with an inquiring smile. She had on a brightly patterned top that made her look even more energetic than usual.

"I, uh, have to apologize."

Ms. Broom looked confused. "About *what?*" she asked.

Sam stared at the floor. "Well, uh, you know how people are being weird around town? Well, like, that's because of me. I got everybody together to make it friendlier for you."

It took a moment or two to really get rolling on his confession. Sam found it scary but still rather satisfying; Ms. Broom certainly was paying attention to him. "But when you said it got too friendly, I tried to fix it? So I went and told some people that you were used to it being more private, but they kind of gossiped, and mixed it up, so it's my fault, and I'm really sorry, but I also figured out how to fix everything."

He pulled a folded sheet of paper from his pocket and handed it to Ms. Broom, who looked at it warily. "We can put this in the paper. I got the idea from J. Earl Goodenough: it's the power of the press. If you say okay, all we have to do is phone them before nine o'clock."

Ms. Broom began to read. A moment later she began to smile. Looking up she said, "Thank you, Sam. I accept your apology. And thanks for trying to make things friendly. Maybe this will *help.*"

"Oh, it will," Sam assured her, "Everybody reads the *Eternal.* And if you want I'll go all over town and tell people, too."

Ms. Broom started. "No! That's okay, Sam. Tell you what. You phone about this, and I'll do the talking for myself when I'm downtown. That way I won't be a new face much longer. *Okay?"*

"Okay!" said Sam, and turned joyfully for the door.

"Oh, and Sam . . ." Ms. Broom hesitated, "the man that was at your house that time—what was his name?" She shuffled pictures for the bulletin board.

"What man?" Sam was mystified. Who could be more memorable than he was?

"Well, he was quite big and friendly, and he had a yellow hat on."

"Smitty?" Sam said.

"Ahhh," said Ms. Broom, "that's it. Thanks." She was maybe not blushing but pink anyway. "I, uh, was wondering because I see him around town, and I couldn't remember his name to say hi. I wouldn't want him to think I was *unfriendly.*"

Sam's feet made a delightfully Trucklike thunder on the stairs. At the bottom he stopped to read the paragraph one more time:

> Welcome to Nancy Broom, grade six teacher at O.P. Doberman School. Freshly moved from Toronto, Nancy reports that she has been overwhelmed by the interest and generosity of Springers since her move here and wishes to thank everyone for their many kindnesses. "I've never lived

in a small town before," she says, "but now I wouldn't want to live anywhere else. I hope I'm fortunate enough to teach here for a long time."

Robin had been especially proud of making up the quote. Sam grinned. Finally, a plan had worked. Special at last, he thought.

He rounded the corner to the office. Darryl and Ian stood by the door. Darryl turned and his face darkened. Then he looked down the hall as if Sam were invisible. Sam stared at the ceiling as he walked past. Behind him, Darryl said something. Ian laughed. Sam stiffened his back, but his insides sagged. Happiness, it seemed, like being special, was not that easy to plan.

17
Back in the Bin

Sam kept away from Darryl. At recess he played wall ball with Amanda. He made sure to laugh and yell as loudly as he could. Sam figured that way, if Darryl had any brains at all, he'd see what a great time he was missing. Darryl, however, always seemed to be playing soccer. You could hear him shouting all the way across the school yard. Sam gritted his teeth thinking about it. It didn't help that he could tell Amanda was letting him win every once in a while.

He tried to cheer himself by thinking how everything was finally coming together to make him a star. Unfortunately, apart from making up for the friendliness plan, he couldn't think of anything in particular that *was* coming together.

"Where's Darryl these days?" Mr. Foster asked Sam in the middle of the week. It was the third day in a row he'd come home to find Sam aimlessly watching TV after he'd done his papers. Amanda had suggested they train for track and field together, but Sam hadn't been in the mood. Now he shrugged.

"You're not turning into a teenager already, are you?" Mr. Foster asked suspiciously, walking on into the kitchen to start supper. Sam didn't bother to answer.

Ms. Broom, meanwhile, was perkier than ever. Thanks to me, Sam told himself, but really he knew Ms. Broom wasn't treating him any differently than before. She even chose Darryl for Student of the Month. Sam fumed. Maybe she was waiting until summer, he thought, to keep his hopes up. It wasn't easy to do.

When Saturday rolled around, Mrs. Foster put Sam to work in the Bulging Bin unpacking bars of coal tar and cucumber soap, a gritty black mixture that matched Sam's mood. The sun was shining, but he had to work his own shift and one he owed Robin. Not that he had anything fun to do anyway, he thought, stacking bars in the soap cabinet. Amanda had gone to Toronto for the Blue Jays game and Darryl—well, it didn't matter anymore what Darryl was doing.

Doing. Sam remembered again what J. Earl had said: "What you do isn't always what you are." He wondered half-heartedly what it had meant. Was it that J. Earl really liked poems better than sounding off? Or that he really didn't like poetry even though he recited it in the woods?

Sam heaved a sigh, inhaling the nose-tickling fragrances of the soap cabinet. Who cared anyway? He thought gloomily about his own doings with newspapers, underwear, cross-country, lottery tickets. . . . The list seemed to go on and on. What good was it knowing he was different from the dumb things he'd done if nobody else did? To everybody else, except maybe Amanda, he was about as spectacular as soap. He looked down at the dull black bar in his hand and sighed again. In Sam's opinion coal tar and cucumber stunk.

The store was busy, so it was almost noon before Mrs. Foster told Sam to get out the broom. The doorbell jingled as more customers came in. One of them was Darryl.

Sam grimaced and hustled off to sweep at the back of the store. Darryl didn't appear to be overjoyed, either. His head jerked around like a chicken pecking, looking everywhere but at Sam.

The Bulging Bin was not large, and Sam was finished at the back a lot faster than he wanted to be. Darryl, on the other hand, was setting a world's record for slowness. There was nothing Sam could do now but aim his broom for wherever Darryl wasn't. Unfortunately, Darryl didn't seem to know where he was going. He plodded up the left aisle to the rice and spaghetti, then turned and started back. Sam had to spin around to avoid him, barely avoiding spearing a lady at the raisin bins. He scuttled around the corner into the store's other aisle. Darryl again. Sam turned, swerved around a stout customer at the coffee grinder and blundered squarely into a display of decorator biscuit tins. The crash as they descended sounded like something from the Canada Day demolition derby. "Gaaah!" Sam shouted and dropped the broom.

In the deathly silence that followed, Sam heard his mom asking, "What are you looking for, Darryl?" in the kind of perfectly calm voice that parents get when they're pretending not to notice their kids blundering around like elephants.

"Chocolate chips," Darryl replied, sounding as if he had never heard of them before in his life.

"Baking supplies," Mrs. Foster said briskly. "Right over by Sam. And the biscuit tins."

People began to move again. Hemmed in by fake-old tins, Sam heard the familiar shuffle of clunky, black hightops behind him.

"They're right there." Sam nodded at the chocolate chips instead of looking at Darryl.

"Uh-huh." Darryl didn't move.

"You getting them or what?" Sam glanced over his shoulder.

"How?" The metal avalanche had blocked Darryl's path.

"What am I supposed to do?" Sam snapped back. "Get them for you?"

"Good idea," Darryl said, "for once."

Sam bristled. "So make me, then."

"I don't make monkeys."

"Since when?"

"Since—"

"Boys." Mrs. Foster's voice carried from the cash register. Now it had the kind of cheery warning note in it that teachers use when they really mean shut up. Mrs. Foster had once been a teacher.

Sam tore a plastic bag off the nearest roll and banged open the bin. "How much?" he said from between clenched teeth.

"I dunno. My mom just said a bag."

Sam scooped some chips into the bag and dropped the lid back down on the bin. Reaching for a twist tie, he hissed, "Just so you know about good plans, I made another one and told it to Ms. Broom and she loved it and now everything's okay and she said it was thanks to me, so thanks for nothing to you."

"Oh yeah?" Darryl hissed back. "So what's she gonna do, marry you?"

Sam could feel himself blushing all the way to his toes. He turned. "Why? Did you think she was gonna marry *you?*"

Darryl's face turned so red his freckles almost disappeared. He snatched the bag of chocolate chips from Sam's hand and spun away. Four shuffling steps later he stopped. "Sam," he called urgently. "Look!"

Sam waded through the biscuit tins to where Darryl was staring out the door. His heart leaped so suddenly he almost fell into the bulk corn chips. "Holy kazoo," he breathed.

Across the street was a stunning scene: Smitty and Ms. Broom stood talking by the fire hydrant. This was not stunning in itself, even though Smitty did look quite tidy, for Smitty. His T-shirt was tucked in and he didn't need a shave. What was stunning was that Smitty and Ms. Broom were holding hands.

"I don't believe it," Sam said.

"Me neither," said Darryl. They watched as Smitty laughed and Ms. Broom flashed one of her colossal smiles, then the two strolled off toward the Four Corners hand in hand.

The boys ran out of the store in time to see the couple turn the corner. "What would she like *Smitty* for?" Darryl squinched his nose in disbelief. His freckles crowded together.

"Beats me," Sam said.

"Maybe she thinks he's rich," Darryl said gloomily.

"Nah," Sam said. "It's probably . . ." His voice trailed off. Smitty was a nice guy, Sam thought, but to tell the truth he couldn't think of a single reason why Ms. Broom would like Smitty *better.* Finally, he said lamely, "Maybe it's just 'cause they're both grownups."

Darryl shook his head. "Weird or what, eh?"

"I guess," Sam said. He didn't like to think of Ms. Broom as weird; maybe just temporarily crazy.

"I always thought she was a little strange," Darryl said.

"You did?" Sam was shocked.

Darryl nodded sagely. "Yeah, just little things. Like, you ever notice how she'd tap one foot while I was talking? It was almost like a code or something. I bet it really means that . . ." He dug some mints out of his pocket and offered one to Sam as he went on with his explanation.

Sam barely listened. He stood in the sunshine, filled with sweet regret. As the warm spring air and the fragrance of the candy enveloped him, he was surprised to find he was also relieved. What if Ms. Broom *had* wanted to marry him? Or even hold hands, for that matter? They were embarrassing thoughts; scary even. Was that really what he had wanted? He'd thought so for a while, but now Sam realized, he'd just been confused.

Really he wanted something grander than that. He wanted Ms. Broom to just somehow think of him as *special.* In fact, he wanted the whole world to think of him that way. He sighed nobly. It was better for Smitty and Ms. Broom to be happy together than for her—and Sam—to have made a terrible mistake. Besides, he was still up on Darryl. After all, which of them was pals with Smitty?

Sam lifted his chin and took a deep, minty breath. Truck Foster was still rolling; he could still find a way to stand out. The new, improved model was yet to come.

Sam's mom leaned out of the store. "Taking early retirement, Sam?" Sam jumped. Darryl stopped explaining.

"I gotta go," Sam said. He started back inside.

"Hey, Sam?" Darryl called. He paused. "What time do you finish?"

It was only now that Sam remembered he wasn't speaking to Darryl any more. He answered anyway. "Three o'clock. Why?"

Darryl picked at a scab on his elbow. "Oh, I dunno."

"Want to go blading or something?" Sam asked, trying not to sound like this was anything special.

"Automatic," Darryl said.

18
SCRUGS

"Okay, we're almost done," said Darryl, checking off streets on his town map. "Now." He squinted thoughtfully through his freckles; in sunny weather he had more of them than ever. Sam and Amanda leaned in, like generals planning a battle. At least Amanda did. Sam was fighting an urgent need to pick his nose.

It was the first week of summer holidays. The days were still filled with the heart-lightening freedom of school's end. Sam, Amanda, and Darryl were huddled around a picnic bench in the town park. Nearby, the Doberman Memorial Band Shell, freshly painted pink and white, gleamed in the morning sun like a giant wedding cake. Sam knew it well: Mr. Foster and his fellow Stompers performed there every Thursday evening in July and August. Right now, however, a huge banner advertised it as the starting point for the coming Hope Springs House and Garden Tour.

Behind the band shell a few teenagers were unlimbering their skateboards and kicking a hackysack, looking bored already. At the benches by the sidewalk, moms and tots and senior citizens were gathering, waiting more or less patiently for the library across the street to open. All in all, it was a typical summer morning in Hope Springs.

"Do these," Darryl pointed to the map. "Then we get paid."

"And then we can go tubing on the river," Amanda put in.

Sam got his finger out of his nose in time to say, "Automatic."

Darryl divided up the streets they had to check. As they set off on their bikes, he called out the usual instructions they didn't need. "Meet at the Bin in an hour," Sam called back. "We can get a drink." He didn't mind if Darryl sounded bossy; they all knew Sam had gotten them the job. Besides, Sam had bigger fish to fry.

Actually it was Robin, who was now writing the "Teen Scene" column for the paper, who had gotten them the job. *The Hope Springs Eternal* was paying them ten dollars each to make a list of all the lawn ornaments in town so a photographer could take pictures of the best ones. Ms. Sedgwick, the editor, said they would make a nice contrast with the photos of expensive antiques and elegant gardens that would be printed after the big house tour on Saturday.

At least that was the part Sam had told the others. What he hadn't told them was the secret reason the *Eternal* wanted the pictures—and why Sam wanted to help. That reason was SCRUGS.

SCRUGS stood for the Society for the Complete Removal of Ugly Garden Statues, a mysterious group that made off with such things in the middle of the night and left them on the town hall lawn. SCRUGS hadn't struck since last year, but Robin had overheard Ms. Sedgwick saying she bet pictures would get SCRUGS going again.

"Why would she want them to?" Sam had asked when Robin told him. "Doesn't she like lawn ornaments?"

"It's not that, you twit! If SCRUGS strikes they can put a story in the paper about it." Since nothing much ever happened in Hope Springs, the paper was always short of stories.

This had given Sam his own idea, one he had so far kept totally secret, despite its brilliance. Step One of this idea was making the list. Now, pedaling the hills across town, Sam knew it was almost time for Step Two. By the time Step Three was done, Sam would be a Somebody.

But first, his last few streets. In practically no time he found and noted a plaster donkey in a straw hat, a Bambi with a pot of geraniums blooming in its back, some elves under a polka dot toadstool, and a fluffy flock of miniature pink sheep with blue bows tied around them. At the end of the last street Sam turned. He had one stop left to make before heading for the Bin.

The fastest route led down Albert Street. As Sam rolled along however, he spotted Cornell Leamish's green plaster gnomes, still unlisted. He braked beneath the red maple and whipped out his notebook, feeling like an ace reporter. Or maybe a master spy; it changed from street to street.

Counting the gnomes, he couldn't help noticing the pool was back in operation. Or rather, it would have been if there had been anyone to swim in it. Sam sighed. It wasn't the first time he'd regretted his misunderstanding with Cornell Leamish. He wished he could tell him what J. Earl had said about what you are not being the same as what you'd done. But now, Sam thought, it was too late.

Sam jotted the address and "5 green nomes." As he finished he noticed J. Earl himself standing on his doorstep. A coffee mug was in his hand, and a disgruntled look was on his face.

"What're you up to now, Foster?"

Sam told him. J. Earl grunted.

"Were you doing thinking work?" Sam asked.

"I was until you interrupted me."

"Sorry," Sam said politely, not sure how he'd interrupted.

"Don't worry about it," said J. Earl, walking over to join him. "I wasn't getting anywhere anyway."

"Are they going to cut down the tree?" Sam asked.

J. Earl chuckled. "Town council hasn't done a thing about it, and I don't care if they ever do." Despite his grumpy expression he seemed surprisingly mellow. This might be a good time to finally find out about the paper, Sam thought. It occurred to him in the same instant that he'd recently heard something about the tree. For the life of him he couldn't remember what it was. Until he could he said, "How come you like trees so much?"

"I think I could turn and live with animals," J. Earl said unexpectedly.

"They are so placid and self-contained,

Not one is dissatisfied. . . .

"Trees are like that, too, Foster. They don't talk and I doubt they listen."

"Is it a poem?" Sam asked hesitantly.

J. Earl nodded. "By Walt Whitman. But who'd know that now? Listen:

"When stately trees I see, barren of leaves

That erst from heat did canopy the herd,

And summer's green all girded up in sheaves

Borne on the bier with white and bristling beard. . . .

"Shakespeare. I'm sixty-six years old, Foster. I like old things. Poems. Small towns. Trees."

Sam wasn't quite sure he understood what the great man was talking about, but this had to be the time. "Hey, Mr. Goodenough," he said, "would you please tell—"

"Anyway, enough about that," J. Earl interrupted. "C'mon in here. Mark this down on your list. In capital letters."

He led Sam over to his garage and pulled up the door. Peering into the dimness Sam made out a small statue in the corner. It was of a little boy who seemed to be about to do something rude that only babies did in public, and even they wore diapers.

"You hook it up to your garden hose," said J. Earl proudly, "and he—well, you get it. Isn't it terrific? It's a copy of a famous fountain in Belgium."

"Wow," Sam said, "but how come it's in here?"

J. Earl chuckled. "I only put it out on House and Garden Tour Day."

"Because you're scared of SCRUGS?" Sam guessed. All lawn ornament owners knew about SCRUGS.

"No! To show the whole town isn't snooty! Listen Foster, that tour is just an excuse for rich people to show off their stuff. Why else would you let a bunch of strangers tramp through your house? That's not good taste!" J. Earl's head was turning pink, a sign that Sam would probably be hearing about this on TV soon. "That's showing off," J. Earl went on, "and I can't stand showoffs."

"My dad says you show off on TV," Sam said, without thinking.

J. Earl stared. "Did you think before you said that? Anyway, that's different. I'm airing the important issues of the day." Indeed, recently, J. Earl had complained about smelly pet food. "And this little gem," J. Earl walked in and patted the little boy on the head, "is my protest against phony good taste."

Sam said, "But I thought you liked your lawn ornament."

"I do," J. Earl said smugly. "I hate it so much I love it."

Sam started to back away. There was no use getting his brain tied up in knots. Still, he did have one last question that J. Earl could answer without anyone else being the wiser.

"If somebody caught SCRUGS," he asked, trying to sound innocently curious, "do you think it would be in the paper?"

"Are you asking me as a media professional?" J. Earl boomed.

"I guess," Sam said, thinking, Whatever that is.

"That would be a good story." J. Earl nodded for emphasis. "Anybody that caught SCRUGS might be looking at national airplay."

"TV?" Sam gulped.

"Absolutely."

"The power of the press, huh?" Sam hurriedly picked up his bike.

"Speaking of which," J. Earl called after him, "when are you going to put my paper in the right place?"

Sam was thinking too hard to answer. His secret idea had been even more brilliant than he thought. Now he had a lot to do.

19
Hilda

With twenty minutes left before he met the others, Sam pedaled to Smitty's as fast as he could. When he arrived, Smitty was preparing to drive over to Ms. Broom's. He was painting her apartment while she taught summer school.

"Hey, Smitty," Sam asked, "is there an old board I can have?" Smitty's garage was filled with odds and ends from projects he'd helped out on. They went in, and Sam found a piece of plywood about a meter and a half high and a meter across.

"What do you want it for?" Smitty asked.

The time had come. "Can you keep a secret?" Sam asked. "I'm gonna catch SCRUGS! I'm gonna cut this and paint it up like a fat lady bending over and stick it in the garden, there'll be a picture in the paper, SCRUGS will come, and, bammo, I'll catch 'em."

"How?" Smitty jingled the change in his pockets.

"I've got this volleyball net." Smitty raised his eyebrows. "Don't worry, I've got it all figured out."

"How are you going to carry the wood home?"

Sam hadn't thought about that.

"Tell you what," Smitty said. "You draw the shape, I'll cut it out and drop it at your place on the way to Nancy's."

"Thanks, Smitty." Sam pulled out his pencil and got to work.

Smitty chuckled. "Hey, if you catch them I get to be a hero, too."

Sam didn't answer. In the back of his mind he still couldn't help wondering just a bit what Ms. Broom might think of him after he'd been on national TV. Maybe she'd tell Sam, "Call me Nancy."

Amanda and Darryl were waiting when Sam got to the Bulging Bin. He pulled out his list, wrote POLKA DOT FAT LADY—REALLY GREAT!! with his own address, and added it to the pile of papers on the counter.

"Hey," said Amanda, "you don't have one of those in your garden."

"I will by this afternoon," Sam said. "I'm already making it."

"You just want a picture in the paper," Darryl scoffed.

"More than that," Sam said. "But I can't tell you."

"Aw, come on, Truck," said Amanda.

"Nope. Hey, Mom," Sam called, "do we have any paint at home?"

"Just what Dad bought for the trim," Mrs. Foster called back.

Sam groaned. He hadn't thought about this, either.

"We have paint at our house," said Amanda, "and brushes."

"So do we," said Darryl temptingly, "lots of colors."

Sam looked helplessly from one to the other. "Okay," he sighed, "can you keep a secret?"

They painted the fat lady that afternoon. She was life-sized, but since she was supposed to be bending over in the garden, you only saw a giant bottom in a red and white polka dot dress, a frill of blue underwear, and two thick legs disappearing into the flowers. Mr. Foster suggested calling her Hilda because she reminded him of an aunt by that name.

Hilda was still a little sticky, but they set her up in the Fosters' front garden anyway, near the tree and under Sam's window. Then they walked out to admire her from the street. Hilda's oversized bottom rose like a giant birthday balloon from the greenery.

"She'll be in the paper for sure," Amanda said.

"Yeah, and how can SCRUGS resist?" Sam gloated.

Darryl nodded. "So, we'll put a rope from the support stick to the volleyball net up in the tree, and we'll tie a bag of tin cans to the net for an alarm bell. One tug on the rope and down comes the net."

"And on comes the light," Sam said, for once adding something to one of Darryl's explanations, "'cause I'll be waiting."

"We'll be waiting," Amanda corrected. She was already set to stay over at Holly's across the street. Darryl would be at Sam's.

"Right," Sam said, hoping they'd fall asleep.

They were interrupted by voices from next door. Sam turned to see his neighbor, Mr. Yates, talking with Mrs. Felice Doberman. Mrs. Doberman, of course, lived in the mansion on Albert Street. She was also the mother of Lyle Doberman, kayaking hunk and towel snapper. Just now, though, she had another role: she was the organizer of the Hope Springs House and Garden Tour. Sam watched as she clipped a tasteful blue sign to Mr. Yates' picket fence. This, combined with a bouquet of balloons, would show his house was on Saturday's tour. The house was a hundred years old, but it looked fresh and new.

Sam glanced at his own house. It looked more like a thousand years old. The trim was blotchy where Mr. Foster had been scraping it. Storm windows were stacked on the front porch for painting, along with a hockey net, Sam's bike, and a couch they hadn't yet hauled away to Really Recycling. The front lawn needed cutting, too. Sam thought a decoration like Hilda made up for it all. He'd gotten quite fond of lawn ornaments even if he did want SCRUGS to strike.

"And stay away all the day long is my advice," Mrs. Doberman was drawling. "Busloads of people come to town for this. It's a daylong stampede. I never go *near* home when our place is on the tour."

"Hi, Mr. Yates," Sam called. "Hi, Mrs. Doberman. See our lady?"

Mr. Yates looked and laughed. "Love her!"

Mrs. Doberman smiled, almost. "Very nice." As she climbed into her Range Rover, Sam heard her say to Mr. Yates, "Heaven help us. Why people put up that trash. . . . I don't know how you put up with it."

Stung, Sam turned away. Amanda, who had also heard Mrs. Doberman, stuck out her tongue. "Let's take the list to Robin," Sam said.

Robin and Marlon were in the park. They were part of a group under the oak trees, where Lyle Doberman was holding court. Sam watched disdainfully as Lyle swept his perfect hair up off his forehead.

"Showing off his zits again," he said to Darryl and Amanda as they approached. Sam was in no mood to be charitable after Mrs. Doberman's comment about Hilda.

Lyle was entertaining everyone with a laughing account of how his mother had come home from Bermuda a day early and found Lyle having a party.

"She went ballistic. Now she says that if I don't smarten up she'll send me to boarding school." Lyle rolled his eyes at this parental childishness. "So I'll have to do something nice to chill her out." Robin giggled and played with her hair on the side of her head where there still was some. Marlon videoed squirrels.

Sam handed his sister the list. "You're supposed to take this to Ms. Sedgwick this aft," he said, "with your 'Teen Scene' stuff. And don't forget to get our money."

Robin did her best to pretend Sam was invisible. "It's a list of every stupid lawn ornament in town," she told everyone.

"Hey," Sam said. He'd had enough of this from Mrs. Doberman.

"Let's see!" The pages started to make their way around the group. Sam grabbed for one and missed. "Bunny rabbits with wind spinner ears," someone read out, "the Seven Dwarfs and a Mr. Wise Old Owl! Man, no wonder SCRAM steals this junk."

"It's SCRUGS," Sam said, grabbing again, "and—"

"Pink sheep!" Lyle Doberman snorted.

"They're just little ones," Sam snapped. "They're pretend," but Lyle was too busy sweeping back his hair to listen. Sam snatched at the paper again. Lyle held it out of reach. Amanda stepped up behind him and grabbed it. Sam looked at her gratefully.

Robin shook her head. "It's affected their brains," she said to Lyle. Sam gave up.

"Just take in the list," he said, and turned to go.

Behind him he heard Lyle say, "I'll give you a drive if you want." Lyle, of course, had his own car.

"Great!" Robin said. Marlon scowled behind his video camera. "POLKA DOT FAT LADY—REALLY GREAT," someone read, as Sam lifted his bike. "Hey, Robin, is that you?"

"That you, Sam? Telephone!" Mr. Foster called as Sam climbed the back steps a little while later. Sam ran inside to find Ms. Sedgwick on the line. She was not happy.

"Sam, where's my list? It was due today."

"Robin's bringing it," Sam explained. "I already gave it to her."

"Well, Robin's been and gone, and she didn't leave it. Can you find out what's going on, please?"

Sam groaned and called Robin at the Bulging Bin.

"I put it in her mail slot," she snapped back over the phone. "Now quit bugging me. A baby just drooled in the macaroni bin."

Sam called Ms. Sedgwick. There was no list in her mail slot. "Write up another one as best you can and get it here fast," she ordered. "We have to run the pictures Friday before pictures from the house and garden tour. That means we take the shots tomorrow. We need that list now, Sam. "

Sam took time out to groan again. Then he called his friends.

When he went to bed that night a new list was at the paper. Robin had continued to insist that she'd left the first one at the newspaper office. Sam had been in such a rush to redo his work that he hadn't had time to argue with her or even wonder how a list could simply vanish. Amanda and Darryl had complained, but not very hard. Having brothers and sisters themselves, they understood that things could go wrong. Besides, they were each ten dollars richer.

Sam turned over in bed and kicked back the cover. It was a warm night. If the pictures would be in the paper Friday, he thought, that would be the night they'd watch for SCRUGS. He imagined leaping outside as the tin cans clanked the alarm. A crowd would gather, all cheering, even though it would be the middle of the night. Ms. Broom would be there, of course, and Smitty and Amanda and Darryl and his other friends and the newspaper photographer and J. Earl and a TV crew and . . .

When Sam awoke the next morning, Hilda was gone. So was every lawn ornament in town.

20
Papers and Papers

The police came around 10:30. The Hope Springs force was not what you'd call large, and they'd had a lot of places to go. Constable Al wrote down Hilda's description. Constable Vern inspected the crime scene. "Do you think it was SCRUGS?" Sam asked.

They shrugged. "We always hear from them when it is," Al said, flipping his notebook shut. "And so far there's nothing on the town hall lawn."

Vern started up the cruiser. "We'll be in touch."

Darryl and Amanda came over. "How could you let her get stolen?" Darryl complained, sharing out some gum. Amanda just chewed thoughtfully. There was nothing else to do.

Then the phone rang. It was Ms. Sedgwick at the *Eternal.*

"Sam, what's with this list? Our photographer can't find a single thing on it!"

"That's 'cause it was all stolen," Sam exclaimed. "They took Hilda and everything! The police were just here."

"Whatwhatwhat?" Ms. Sedgwick's tone shifted from impatience to interest. "When? Tell me what you know." Sam told what he could. "Great!" Ms. Sedgwick crowed. "Now, get me Robin."

Sam found himself caught up in Ms. Sedgwick's energy. He just wished she didn't sound so happy about it. He clunked down the receiver. "Raaaw–binnnnn."

The bathroom door opened and Robin stalked out, her head wrapped in a bath towel. She had been renewing the orange on the hairy side of her head. "What is it?"

"Phone. Ms. Sedgwick."

Robin brightened and took the receiver. "Hello?" It didn't take long for Robin to get energized, too. "Okay," she said, quickly. "Okay. Sure." She grabbed a pencil and began writing. "And then do you want me to—? Oh." Robin's shoulders sagged. "Okay. Bye."

"Whatta ya gotta do?"

Robin sighed. "I have to go interview these people about what got stolen. Then I have to hand in my notes so someone 'more experienced' can write the story." She pursed her lips in exasperation. "I could write that story. She never lets me write anything special." Sam watched in surprise as Robin slouched away.

The police hadn't called by the time Sam started his papers that afternoon. By now, he knew, Hilda could be firewood. Or maybe she'd be held for ransom. And either way his chance to be a hero was gone. He probably wouldn't get mentioned in the paper, either. Sam tried not to think about any of it.

When he arrived at the Dobermans', he saw a tasteful blue House Tour sign had been staked into the lawn. Mrs. Doberman, in a huge straw hat with cloth daisies on it, was doing some pre-tour fussing in her garden. Kneeling under the gigantic hat, she looked like a large lawn ornament herself. A mushroom, perhaps.

"Sam," she called, "grab those papers there, would you?"

Some advertising flyers had nestled under a forsythia bush. "Sure," he called back. Mrs. Doberman turned back to her work.

Sam reached under the bush, his carrier bag dragging beneath him like an extra stomach, and snagged the papers with his fingertips. They separated as they came out and Sam stopped breathing. Crumpled in with the flyers was a page of the missing list. Sam grabbed it. His first instinct was to run to the nearest person. He looked up. The nearest person was the mushroom-domed Mrs. Doberman. Think, J. Earl had said. Sam hesitated, then stuffed everything into his carrier bag and hurried down the hill.

J. Earl answered Sam's knock, and for once he had his glasses on.

"Mr. Goodenough," Sam said, holding out the list, "look at this. It's a clue!"

J. Earl looked. "You should fold things when you put them in your pockets, Foster. Crumpled up like this, it's a mess."

"I didn't crumple it," Sam exclaimed, "SCRUGS did! Don't you see? It's part of our missing list! SCRUGS must have stolen it somehow, and they dropped it maybe when they were taking the Mitchells' plastic raccoons over there. I've gotta take it to the police."

"What are you talking about?" J. Earl squinted over his bifocals.

"Haven't you heard?" Sam was stunned. "Every lawn ornament in town is gone!"

"What the—" J. Earl said several surprising words he never used on TV and rushed for his garage. The rude little boy was still there.

"They took them last night?" said J. Earl angrily. "And everyone thinks it's SCRUGS?"

"Who else would it be?" Sam asked.

"I don't know," J. Earl said, "but it wasn't SCRUGS. *I'm* SCRUGS and I didn't do it."

Sam stared. "You're—"

"Who else?" J. Earl said. "Someone's gotta be."

"Why?"

"Some other time," said J. Earl. "Right now I wanna know who took this stuff. Forget the cops—*I'm* not having SCRUGS blamed."

"But if SCRUGS didn't do it, it could be anybody!"

"Hardly!" J. Earl snorted. He plucked the paper from Sam's grasp. "This is the list you were making yesterday? And it went missing? Tell me about it. Everything, right from the beginning."

Sam told him. The story seemed to grow on its own as he went along until it included Darryl and Amanda, Robin, Lyle, Mr. Yates, Mrs. Doberman, and, of course, Hilda. Sam wondered if this was what happened to Darryl when he explained things.

"All right," said J. Earl when Sam was finished. "First of all, we're looking for someone who doesn't like lawn ornaments." Sam and J. Earl looked at each other. Then they looked back up the Albert Street hill to the mansion. "Mrs. Doberman?" Sam's voice was squeaky with astonishment.

J. Earl looked doubtful. "I wouldn't put it past her. But did she know you were making a list?"

Sam shook his head.

"All right then. Someone who doesn't like lawn ornaments and who knew about the list."

"And," Sam added, "who knew it was going to be at the paper so they could go there and steal it."

"Good point," J. Earl nodded. "So. Any suggestions?"

"Well . . ." Sam said, "no."

J. Earl looked disgusted.

"All the kids in the park knew." Sam tried again.

"But it disappeared right away. They didn't go to the paper."

Sam's head snapped up. The hairs on the back of his neck prickled. "Lyle Doberman did." He fought down a rising tide of excitement to speak slowly and clearly. "How about," Sam said, "if it was somebody who needed to make their *mom* who didn't like lawn ornaments happy? *And* who knew about the list *and* was at the newspaper office *and* has their own car?"

J. Earl looked steadily at Sam for a moment. One massive eyebrow arched like a hawk, high on his forehead, as he considered. Then he smiled the way he did when he got off an especially upsetting comment on TV.

"Bingo." He took the paper from Sam and dropped it into

the blue recycling box. The smile broadened into a grin. "Let's get busy," he rasped. "This means war."

As Sam followed him in, something made him glance across the lawn. Cornell Leamish stood in his garden, giving Sam a suspicious glare.

21
Council of War

Sam had never seen Smitty's living room as crowded as it was that night; in fact he'd never even seen it used before. Smitty, Uncle Dave, J. Earl, and Ms. Broom were sitting in the plastic chairs from the patio table set Smitty used in the dining room. Robin and Marlon were slouched on the futon. Since there were no other seats, Amanda and Darryl were on the carpet beside the TV. In front of them was Thursday's *Eternal,* its banner headline proclaiming: LAWNS STRIPPED IN STUNNING HEIST. Through the open window drifted wisps of Dixieland music. Mr. Foster and his fellow Stompers were performing down at the band shell.

Sam was standing beside Smitty's new exercise bicycle, feeling embarrassed as he stumbled through his theory about Lyle Doberman for the group. Darryl had offered to explain for him, but Sam had said no. He hadn't wanted to miss a guaranteed chance to be special in front of everyone. Now, unfortunately, he was discovering that public speaking wasn't the way he wanted to be special. Finally, J. Earl came to his rescue.

"So Lyle Doberman gets in trouble for throwing a party and wants to please his mommy again," J. Earl clarified things from his chair, "and he discovers the way when the kids show up with their list. Felice Doberman wants this town neat as a pin for her house tour, and we know she hates lawn ornaments. So what does her loving son do?"

"Steals them," said Marlon. It was the first time Sam could

remember him speaking, and his voice was surprisingly deep. Robin's face was crimson.

"Exactly," J. Earl trumpeted. "He pretends to do Robin a favor by offering her a ride"—here Marlon snorted and Robin picked at the hole in the knee of her jeans—"but really he's out to steal the list, which he does when Robin gives him a tour of the newsroom. *Then* as a surprise for his mom, the little creep lifts every last lawn ornament he can find."

"Do you think his mother *knows?"* Ms. Broom asked. Sam hadn't seen much of her since school ended. While she looked as fetching as ever, she also looked stunned by this saga of small-town larceny.

Sam, Amanda, Darryl, Robin, and Marlon all shook their heads at once. They were, after all, the experts on dealing with parents. "You wouldn't tell about it until it worked and it was all done," Darryl said, "'cause afterward they'd think it was fun if it went okay. But if it didn't and you'd already told, you'd really be in trouble. Like, what if the cops found the stuff before the house tour? Know what I mean? Or, like, say you—"

"He hasn't told yet," Amanda summed up impatiently, "if he's smart."

"Who said he was smart?" Marlon muttered. Robin looked at the ceiling.

"Okay, okay," Uncle Dave said. "The point is, what do we do?"

This part Sam could handle. "Well," he nodded at Amanda and Darryl, "we have an idea."

"We trap him," Darryl jumped in again. "See, we were planning to trap SCRUGS? And we had this volleyball net, and we—"

"Darryl," Amanda sighed, "put a cork in it. Let Sam tell."

Sam looked at her gratefully. It seemed to him he was doing that a lot lately. "See, we were going to use Hilda, this lawn statue we made. But now there's only one ornament left in town—"

"Which happens to be mine," J. Earl put in proudly.

Sam nodded. "So we thought we could use it for a trap instead."

Ms. Broom looked worried. "This is nothing against the *law,* is it?"

J. Earl laughed as if that were the silliest thing he'd ever heard. "Would I do anything that would get me in trouble?"

Ms. Broom frowned. "It's getting *us* in trouble that worries me," she said. "I'm new here, but I know how people *talk*. I don't even want to *know* about this. I'll just go sit outside."

"That's fair enough," J. Earl agreed. "I think we all understand." The others all nodded, except Sam, who found himself a little surprised and a little disappointed, too.

"Now," Smitty said. "How?"

Sam said, "We set up the lawn statue where it's easy to steal, and we make sure Lyle knows about it. Then we watch tomorrow night to see who takes it. Marlon videos them for evidence; we grab 'em."

"No, wait!" said Amanda, jumping up with a fresh idea. "Instead of grabbing them, we can *follow* them. Maybe they'd lead us to the other stuff. We could rescue it and be double heroes."

"Yessss!" Sam crowed. Without thinking he gave Amanda a high five. Her face turned pink.

"Which gives me an idea, too." J. Earl said slowly. His eyebrows swooped dramatically as he pulled his chair forward. Everyone leaned toward him as he explained. "To pull it off," he finished, "we'll need everybody. Who's in?"

"I am," from Sam, Amanda and Darryl. It was their plan, after all. "Me, too," Marlon said.

"Me three." Smitty was grinning from his patio chair.

Uncle Dave gave a thumbs up.

J. Earl turned. "I think we need Robin to get the ball rolling. Whaddya say, Robin?"

"Will we get Lyle in trouble for sure?" Robin asked.

"Absolutely guaranteed," J. Earl said. "His mommy will probably make him stay in till he eats his car."

"I'm in," Robin said.

22
The Leamish Factor

At noon on Friday Smitty lugged the rude little boy out to a part of J. Earl's lawn where the streetlight would shine on it. J. Earl hooked up the hose from the same faucet Sam had broken back in the fall. Sam turned on the tap. There was a hissing noise, then a graceful arc of water shot from the little boy and began to splash into a shell-shaped basin. Sam was embarrassed.

"It's practically a work of art," J. Earl enthused.

"It's something," Smitty agreed as he and Sam climbed back into his truck. "We'll see you later."

They drove next to the Cuppa Cafe, where Robin used the pay phone to call Lyle Doberman. Taking a deep breath, she asked was he going to the movies that night with everybody, and by the way had he seen the incredibly sick lawn ornament over at J. Earl Goodenough's. "What a barfbag," she said as she hung up.

Afterward, Sam walked back to the pickup with Smitty. Smitty was headed for Ms. Broom's to paint, and on the way he was going to drop Sam off at the Fosters' house. Darryl and Amanda were waiting to go tubing.

The truck was parked in front of the food bank. Smitty glanced at it as he settled into the driver's seat. Then he tapped the steering wheel lightly with his open palm.

"That's what I keep meaning to ask," he said. He put the key in the ignition. "Few months back, I got a receipt from the

food bank for a hundred and forty-dollar donation. 'Cept I hadn't given 'em any money. So I phoned, an' they said some cash with my name had come through the mail slot one day back in February. You know anything about it?" Smitty reached back casually for his seat belt.

Sam looked away to the door of the food bank and the memory of the storm came swirling back. For a second he felt the cold pavement beneath his knees again and the stiffness of the hinged flap over the letter slot. For some reason he also felt embarrassed at being found out. "Um, geez, I dunno," he shrugged, still looking out the window. "I don't remember."

"Whadja do it for?" The buckle on Smitty's seat belt clicked. "Thought you wanted skates."

Sam shrugged again. "I did. It was just I didn't need all that. You know," he squirmed for a way to avoid sounding syrupy, "I mean, it would have been . . . *boring.*" He risked a glance at Smitty, worried that the last part had sounded rude.

But Smitty was laughing. He took off his ridiculous yellow golf hat and gave Sam a swat, then turned and started up the engine. "Well, thanks, Sammy," he said as he put the truck in gear. "I figured I could count on ya."

The compliment kept Sam glowing even when the river ran cold.

By suppertime Sam was aching with impatience. Mr. Foster served up something in tomato sauce that tasted suspiciously like eggplant. Sam looked at Robin and puffed out his cheeks as if he were going to be sick. Their dad's cooking was one of the few things they agreed on.

Robin put off eating for a moment to ask if she and Sam could go to Uncle Dave's that night. "We'll be really late, but he'll bring us home." She used the story they had agreed on. "We're going worm picking with him and Smitty. At a golf course. Thirty-five cents a pound."

"You're doing something together?" Mrs. Foster was amazed.

"Don't worry," Robin said, "it's a big golf course."

Uncle Dave picked them up in the Hope Springs Hydro van just before dark. Next they called for Darryl and Amanda, also masquerading as worm pickers. When they finally reached J. Earl's, Sam saw Smitty's truck parked up the street. Uncle Dave coasted to a stop under the maple. Everyone but him scuttled out and around the house.

Marlon was already in the back yard setting up his video camera. The great man himself stood guard, wearing a toque to keep the streetlight from reflecting off his head. The house was dark. "My wife's gone to her sister's for the weekend," he informed everyone, "so we'll keep this little caper strictly need-to-know."

"What do we need to know?" Sam asked.

"No, no, no," J. Earl said, "it means—"

Marlon interrupted. "This isn't going to work," he said. "I can't get a good shot from here. We'll have to move."

He pointed across the lawn to the shadows by the Leamish pool.

"We can't go there!" Sam hissed.

"We'll have to," said J. Earl. He tugged down on his toque. "C'mon, and keep it quiet."

With J. Earl in the lead, they began to creep across the lawn. They were almost at the pool when a flashlight beam caught J. Earl square in the face. "GAAH!" he shouted.

Cornell Leamish popped up from behind his pool fence. "I thought you were up to something. You stole my gnomes, didn't you? What were you going to do to my pool?"

J. Earl began to splutter furiously.

"I'm calling the police," said Cornell Leamish.

"No, wait," Sam cried.

"You keep quiet," Cornell Leamish snapped. "I know you."

"You don't understand," said another voice. "We're trying to rescue your gnomes." Darryl stepped forward.

"I wasn't born yesterday, young man," Cornell Leamish scoffed.

Darryl shook his head. "Just listen." And then he explained. Sam had to admit to himself that he did a good job of it, too. "Wait and see, if you don't believe us," Darryl finished. "Only just let us stay." The others all nodded.

"Well," Cornell Leamish hesitated, "if I get my gnomes back, all right, but I'm staying, too—to keep an eye on you."

Everyone breathed a sigh of relief. Amanda poked Sam in the ribs. Sam gave her a thumbs up. Darryl shared out caramels.

They settled down to wait. After a few minutes Cornell Leamish said pointedly, "If that tree wasn't there we'd see a lot better."

"If that tree wasn't there," J. Earl growled, "we wouldn't have any shadows to hide in, would we?"

"Well, if there weren't any shadows I'd have seen someone stealing my gnomes," Cornell Leamish snapped back, louder.

"Oh, is that so?" J. Earl's voice rose angrily. "Well, it just so happens—"

Sam looked at the two bickering men in disbelief. The pale blobs of their faces framed the dark tree and the parked Hydro van. He remembered something. "It just so happens," Sam announced, "that your stupid tree is on town land, so it doesn't belong to either of you, and you're going to wreck everything if you don't keep quiet. Please."

The two grownups were stunned into a momentary silence. Sam was as startled with himself as they were. He was even more startled to see Robin give him what could only have been called a smile.

Then J. Earl rumbled, "Who says?"

"Uncle Dave. He works for Hydro and he knows. You can ask him."

"But right now," Robin put in, "*please* be quiet."

Sam smiled back as an uneasy silence fell. "Thanks," he whispered.

"No problem. We're in the middle of a major story here. *I'm* gonna write it, and I'm not gonna let those two bozos wreck it."

Mosquitoes accompanied the uneasy silence. Darryl ran out of caramels. The ground grew uncomfortably damp. Sam yawned; the rude little boy tinkled away under the streetlight. Once in a while a passing car would slow as its surprised driver took a better look at J. Earl's masterpiece. Marlon practiced by filming them. Then, "Somebody's coming!" Robin warned.

Sam squashed himself flat to the ground. Marlon steadied the camera. Something moved near the tree, then Lyle Doberman scurried out, unhooked the hose on the fountain and dashed away. A moment later his car rolled up, lights off and trunk open. He hopped out and wrestled the fountain inside.

"Not very strong for a hunk," Sam whispered.

"Tell me about it," Robin agreed.

Panting a little, Lyle closed the trunk and hopped back in his car. When he was a block away, Smitty started the truck and swung out to follow. "C'mon," Sam cried. They dashed for the Hydro van, Marlon stumbling along with the camera and tripod, and J. Earl and Cornell Leamish keeping up remarkably well. The rear doors of the van were already open. As they tumbled in Sam thought he heard another car start up as well. Then the doors slammed shut and they pulled away.

It wasn't a long ride. Lyle drove to the band shell and parked around back. The van rolled on by and glided to a stop at the far side of the park. Smitty was further up the street. They watched as Lyle hauled J. Earl's fountain up the back steps of the band shell and into the room behind the stage. A few moments later he scurried out empty-handed and drove away. Smitty followed him. Uncle Dave twirled his Hope Springs Hydro master keys. "Let's have a look," he said.

They climbed the steps to the back room of the band shell. Uncle Dave unlocked the door. Sam found himself walking on tiptoe. Flashlights swept the shabby room. Sam knew it well from the times he had been in here with his dad and the Stompers. Now the rickety table and old stacking chairs were heaped with signs and flyers for tomorrow's house tour. There was no sign of the rude little boy, or any other lawn ornament, for that matter.

"Nothing," said Cornell Leamish. "He's tricked us."

"Hogwash," said J. Earl, "We all saw him carry it in. There's gotta be someplace else."

He shone his flashlight on the bare ceiling.

"Beats me," Uncle Dave said. "I've never been in here before."

Sam was paralyzed with disappointment. The others were talking, but he didn't hear. Amanda said something. Sam didn't listen. She whacked him in the ribs. *"Sam!"* He started. "C'mon Sam, we've gotta *win* this thing. You've been here before. Think!"

Amanda stamped her foot with a frustration that rattled the floorboards. "Ow!" she said, "I stepped on—"

Sam didn't hear the rest; he didn't have to. "I forgot," he cried. "There's a space under the floor."

Everyone crowded around. The flashlight revealed that Amanda had stamped on the hasp of a trapdoor. There was no lock. Uncle Dave swung the big panel up on its hinges, uncovering the crawl space below. The flashlight beams poked down into the gloom. At first they lit up nothing but gravel. Then the lights were dancing eerily over an entire town's worth of lawn ornaments: elves, jockeys, spinners, planters, sheep, the rude little boy, and there, in a corner, "Hilda!" Sam breathed.

"Let's get at it," Uncle Dave whispered. He started down into the hole.

Smitty arrived while they were loading ornaments into the van. Lyle, he reported, had gone straight home. Then he began loading the pickup as well. When both trucks were full there were still ornaments to spare.

"We'll have to make another trip," Uncle Dave said.

"We're pushing our luck now," said Smitty. "We don't want to be caught with this stuff."

That was when the car pulled in, freezing everyone in the glare from its headlights. The lights went off, the motor stopped. Out stepped Ms. Broom.

"Any left? They can go in here." She opened the hatchback.

"What are you doing?" asked Smitty.

"Keeping an eye on all of you," she said.

"But—" Sam began.

Ms. Broom cut him off. "I decided if I was going to live in this town, I might as well live here. But that doesn't mean I want to get *arrested*. Now, hurry up!"

They were finished in no time. Smitty lashed a tarp over the open back of his pickup in case anyone passed them on the way. Ms. Broom spread a blanket over her cargo. Then everyone piled in as best they could for the drive back to J. Earl's.

Sure enough, as they neared Albert Street, a Hope Springs police cruiser came toward them. Sam held his breath. Uncle Dave waved casually. Al and Vern waved back as they rolled by. "Late for coffee at Donut Delight," Uncle Dave said. Sam started to breathe again. He noticed the others did, too.

At J. Earl's they popped Marlon's video into the VCR. The picture was murky, but for a moment it was definitely Lyle you saw under the streetlight, struggling with J. Earl's fountain.

J. Earl checked his watch. "Ten to one," he said. "We all need some sleep. Be back at seven sharp. It's going to be a busy morning."

23
Morning Glory

Sam was dreaming that Hilda was wearing in-line skates and racing after Lyle Doberman with a five-pound bag of baking soda. Sam's own feet were stuck in the peanut butter vats from the Bulging Bin, and he was clumping very slowly up the street after them. Then the sun was streaming in and Robin was shaking him. "Sam! Time to go."

By 7:01 everyone was at J. Earl's. By 7:15 Mr. and Mrs. Doberman had driven off to a busy day of running the house tour. Robin was bouncing on her combat-booted toes at J. Earl's door, clutching the video cassette. Marlon was double-checking his camera while Sam, Amanda, and Darryl were waiting right behind. It was time for J. Earl's part of the plan.

"Let's go," Marlon said, and they dashed up the hill to the Doberman mansion. Amanda got there first and began to ring the bell. Sam pounded on the door as hard as he could. Darryl joined in. An extremely sleepy Lyle Doberman finally answered just as the trucks arrived.

Marlon's camera began to whir. "Lyle," Robin said, in a voice that sounded amazingly like her own mom's, "you're going to watch something. And then you're going to loan us a hose."

Smitty and J. Earl were already unloading little pink sheep. Lyle gaped, and Robin hustled him back into the house before he could even get his mouth closed. Marlon stayed at her shoulder, filming. Sam turned to help at the truck. "If you don't," he heard Robin threaten, "we'll show this video of you to the cops instead."

Faced with a choice between the police and telling his mom he'd been out back all day and never noticed a thing, Lyle Doberman did the sensible thing, which was why the Dobermans' vast front lawn was quickly filled with an entire town's worth of garden ornaments to greet the crowds of house tourists. Elves peeked from the bushes, families of plastic bunnies frolicked on the lawn with herds of little pink sheep, deer with flowerpots in their backs grazed under the trees near giant polka dotted toadstools. A long line of wind spinners wound up the edge of the drive, roadrunners chased squirrels chasing cats chasing tweety birds chasing pinwheels to a chubby pink windmill near the front door. On either side of it, plaster barefoot boys were fishing from ornamental chairs. And in the center of it all, basking in the sunshine was the rude little boy, hard at work before an audience of green garden gnomes. He turned out to be popular with photographers. In fact, some people never made it into the house, they were so fascinated with the lawn. The only thing missing was Hilda: J. Earl had borrowed her for the day for his house.

Everyone was gathered at the Leamish pool when Mr. and Mrs. Doberman returned home at the end of the day to host their annual after-tour party. Mrs. Doberman's roar sounded all the way down the block: "LLLLLLLYYYYYYYLLLLLLE!"

"Do you think he's in trouble?" Robin asked

"I think he's going to boarding school," Marlon replied. They slung their arms over each other's shoulders. Two orange heads bonked softly together. It looked nice with their Aggressive Microwaves PEAS ON EARTH T-shirts, Sam thought. If you liked that kind of stuff.

J. Earl and Cornell Leamish clinked glasses. It had turned out they'd both served in the navy during the war. "There's nothing as downright stupid as a house tour," J. Earl said with satisfaction.

"Couldn't agree with you more," said Cornell Leamish.

The two had been quite chummy ever since they'd had a quiet chat with Uncle Dave earlier in the afternoon.

Everyone else was in the heated, shadowed water, jumping hard as they tried to keep a beach ball in the air. As the game splashed off to one end of the pool, Ms. Broom paused beside Sam.

"Sam," she said, "this may be none of my *business,* but I've got some top secret information for you."

Sam stared.

"Well, maybe not so top secret." Ms. Broom smiled. "I'm not sure if you've noticed or not, but Amanda really likes you."

Sam opened his mouth. Nothing came out.

"Don't let on to anyone I *told.* And don't be embarrassed. I need you *both* for cross-country this fall!" Then, "Over *here!"* Ms. Broom shouted, and with a splash she was gone. Sam took a deep breath and sank underwater.

Down in the silence, he considered. The idea of Amanda liking him was embarrassing as all get out. It was also sneakily, secretly, nice. This was mostly, he suddenly realized, because he liked her, too.

Was this why Amanda picked him first for hockey, even though he wasn't the best? Why she'd wanted to run cross-country together? Why she let him win at wall ball? Why she called him Truck when nobody else bothered? Why she had the exact same Leafs sweater he did? He'd thought it was just because she'd beaten everybody and needed someone to play with. Something warm began to expand inside his chest. Maybe he *was* . . .

It was odd, though. Apart from the glow in his chest, he still mostly felt a lot like plain old Sam Foster. It was all the others, up there in the air, who really seemed special to him: Amanda, Smitty, J. Earl, Ms. Broom, Darryl. . . . Could they really think of him the same way? Sam felt full to bursting. It wasn't emotion; he was out of air. He shot up to the surface in time to hear J. Earl proclaiming, "—a paper unless I'm in it." The grownups roared. Sam gulped more air and sank happily back into the quiet. When he came up again, he finally understood something else. It hadn't taken anything special. All he'd really needed was to do nothing long enough to think.

Monday afternoon Sam set off with his carrier bag over his shoulder. He was walking. He delivered the Dobermans' paper with barely a glance at their now empty lawn, then strode determinedly toward J. Earl Goodenough's.

The enormous hydro truck was parked out front. A lineman was aloft in the cherry picker, sawing a limb from the red maple tree. Several others lay on the ground. Large patches of sunlight now sparkled on the waters of the swimming pool.

Nearby were J. Earl, Cornell Leamish, and Uncle Dave.

"Anywhere there's no sidewalk, that's town land a meter in," Uncle Dave was saying. "We'll clear the branches obstructing the hydro lines, and the rest of the tree is fine. It's a good thing Sam brought it to my attention." He winked at Sam.

"Hear, hear," said Cornell Leamish. Sam handed him his paper; Cornell Leamish's subscription had been renewed.

J. Earl looked at Sam expectantly. Sam looked at J. Earl. Then he marched to J. Earl's front porch and put the paper straight into the recycling box.

"FINALLY!" The sound was so loud Sam jumped. He turned around and J. Earl was beaming. "By golly, Foster, you finally put the paper in the right place. All this time I've been trying to tell you—"

"No, you haven't," said Sam. "I've been trying to ask *you.*"

"Have not," said J. Earl.

"Have too," Sam replied. "But you never listen—you just change the subject."

J. Earl stared at him for a long moment. Sam wondered if he'd gone too far. "Are you trying to tell me to think before I talk?" J. Earl finally asked.

Sam paused and thought. "I guess I am," he said, "sometimes."

"It's a darn good idea," admitted J. Earl. "My wife suggests it all the time." Then he cocked an eyebrow. "Not everybody could tell me that, Foster. But you made one mistake. If you're such a hot listener, when do I read the paper?"

"When you're in it."

J. Earl pointed to Cornell Leamish's paper. Spread across the front page was a banner photo of the decorations on the Doberman's lawn. The caption read: SCRUGS STRIKES AGAIN. The article underneath was by-lined *Robin Foster.*

Sam retrieved the paper from the blue box. J. Earl opened it to admire the picture. Oddly, he didn't seem to need his glasses.

"You know," he said, "I haven't had that much fun in years. We're gonna have to do this again sometime."

"Automatic," Sam said, shaking J. Earl's hand. Not a big deal, he thought. But it was special just the same.